HER SAVAGE,
His Addiction
2

A NOVEL BY

TAYE STORM

ACKNOWLEDGMENTS

First and Foremost, I would like to thank my Heavenly Father. I'm forever grateful that I've been blessed with the gift of creativity. Without Him, I wouldn't have had the courage to continue to explore the craft of writing. I can't thank Him enough for blessing me so much on this journey. Secondly, I'd like to thank my mom who introduced me to urban and erotic fiction novels. I miss the times where we used to spend reading together; I hope I made you proud. Sleep in Peace. I want to thank my dad, for always supporting me. I thank you for being the rock in our family. To my baby sis Worm, thank you for always keeping me laughing and always being a headache. LOL. I hope I inspire you to continue pushing towards greatness. I also want to thank my grandma for your wisdom, your strength, and always being there for me. I love each and every one of you so much.

A huge thank you to Porscha Sterling and the rest of the Royalty family, for welcoming me into your Kingdom. Words cannot express how much of a dream come true this is for me. I'm going to work hard to make you proud.

A big shout out to all of my 8th North family at LMC who read my book and supported me in the beginning stages and purchased a copy, especially: Denise Richardson, Emily Catazaro, Khalifa Lewis, Rebecca Scott, Pam Walker, Sarah Gardner, Bria Riley, Danyelle Riley, Helena Rushin, Chambree Way, Shamika Green, Chrystal Davis and Latoyra Hamilton.

Also, a special thank you Shiryl Davis who has been my test reader since day one. Thank you so much for believing in me. And Tucora Norman for taking time out of your busy schedule to give me feedback. Also to Bethany Williams, thank you for everything you've done to help me during my journey. Lastly, to Tisha Andrews I want to thank you for your friendship, for sharing your wisdom, and for every time you've offered me a word of encouragement.

DEDICATION

I dedicate this book to everyone who took the time to read my first release. Whether you left a positive or negative review, you're appreciated just the same. After seeing the overwhelming response from you guys wanting to read more about Chains and RayVen, I had to make this sequel happen. I thank each and every one of you for your support.

CONNECT WITH ME ON SOCIAL MEDIA.

Facebook: Taye Stroman

IG: @tayestorm0919

PROLOGUE

New Jersey Federal Prison

Newark, New Jersey

 anolo can't fight the smile spreading across his face when he hears the emergency alarms begin to go off overhead. He glances at the clock on the wall where the minute hand ticks to 3AM. "Right on time," he says to himself, as he climbs up from the bed, patiently waiting for the next phase of his plan to come into play.

The echo of automatic gunshots in the distance radiates through the halls, which generates a chorus of screaming and yelling. A tell-tale sign that all hell is breaking loose inside the prison. A few minutes later, the sound of the lock switching on his cell greets his ears, and the door slides open. Without hesitation he gladly steps out into the chaotic scene. Unfortunately, whoever opened his cell had also unlocked the cells of the dozens of other prisoners on the block. There is no telling how long this moment of freedom will last, so the prisoners wasted no time attacking the guards and each other. A wild collection of bullets, clothing, and bleeding bodies left a trail of carnage on the concrete floor. Manolo eventually looks up from the madness to notice two dudes dressed in all-black, seemingly waiting for him at the end of the hall.

"Date prisa!" one of them yells at him, causing him to take off in their direction.

They toss Manolo his bag of personals when he finally catches up with them, and they make their way towards the exit. Only a few feet separated them from executing a perfectly planned escape. However, Warden Johnson jumps in front of them with a shotgun in hand. They pause, only to survey their surroundings for any other opposition. The Warden must have been out of his mind to think he could take them down solo.

"You don't want to do this, Vargas!" he tells them. "Just go back to lock up and we can sort this shit out in the morning."

Manolo drops his head, seemingly thinking over the Warden's offer. However, the sly grin spreading across his face proved otherwise. He nods at the armed man on the right.

"Matalo," he tells him

The man nods back and without hesitation, fires a few shots, catching the Warden in the chest. The sight of him lying on the floor, shirt covered in blood and gasping for air, is enough to make Manolo's dick hard. For years he's waited for the opportunity to make the Warden pay for fucking up the operation he had going. Although Manolo would love to watch him suffer, he can't take a chance on him surviving this shit. He snatches a gun from one of his boys and aims it at the Warden.

"You won't...cough...cough...get away with this, Vargas,"

Warden Johnson says as he fights for breath.

Manolo raises the barrel of the gun to the Warden's head. "Fuck you, Puto!" He squeezes the trigger, shooting him point blank between the eyes. The sight of his brains oozing out onto the floor below, is all the confirmation he needs. To add insult to injury, he spits on the Warden's lifeless body.

"Vamonos!" The dude on the left pats him on the back and they head out the front door.

They keep running until the black Expedition on the other side of the gate becomes visible, and they waste no time jumping inside. With the alarms continuing to sound off outside, it was only a matter of time before the police show up. Once everyone is situated, the driver hauls ass down the road.

"What took you so long, Manny?"

Manolo looks up to see his uncle sitting next to him. Dude is dressed in all-black and puffing on a cigar. He'd been so focused on getting on the other side of those gates, that he hadn't noticed him until now.

"I had to take care of…that bitch ass Warden," he says, still trying to catch his breath.

He shakes his head at his wayward nephew. "You always insist on doing shit the hard way. It's not enough that I just helped you escape a federal prison."

Manolo sneers. "Unc, miss me with that bullshit. That muthafucka always tried to play me, knowing I couldn't lay hands on his ass. I had a chance to clap, so I bodied him. At least I won't have to worry about his ass snitching on me."

"Dumb ass, you just murdered a high-ranking government official in cold blood. You do realize this makes you a walking target. Or did you forget about the cameras?"

"I thought that's what these fools were for," Manolo says pointing at the henchmen.

"They got you out, didn't they?" He shakes his head again and passes Manolo a drink. "I hope you're more careful with handling this dude Chains you told me about."

It's no secret that Manolo hated Chains Verano with a passion. For years, he and his crew Los Lobos brought a reign of terror inside those prison walls. Anything they wanted, they took, no questions asked. That is, until Chains brought his wanna be pretty boy ass on his turf. It's a little-known fact that Manolo and Chains were from the same neighborhood. Maybe because Chains was too arrogant to notice niggas who he didn't think were on his level. Manolo always resented that Chains became Don Armateo's right hand instead of him. Like what the fuck was so special about him? Ever since then, you couldn't tell that nigga he wasn't the shit, which got worse when word spread about how Chains bodied four dudes solo, his first night on the inside. Then muthafuckas started gassing the fool up, acting like they were afraid of him or some shit. Get the fuck outta here.

Manolo tried hard as he could to keep his cool, even though nobody seemed to be pressed over him or his crew anymore. Everything suddenly revolved around Chains. He put up with it as long as he could, until one night that muthafucka stuck his nose in his business. Manolo and a few of his boys had escaped lock up and were on their way out. That is, until he saw that fine ass therapist all alone in the hallway. What was her name? Oh yeah, RayVen. Fine ass RayVen Winds. But seems like she was hooked on Chains' ass. That was another thing that pissed him off. Seems like the muthafucka always had some fly ass bitch coming to the prison to see his ass. He couldn't put nobody else on to a little something to smash. Nah, that muthafucka only cared about himself. So if he couldn't get put on, he'd take what he wanted—starting with RayVen.

Since there was a good chance of them getting caught, Manolo thought it would be a good idea for his homies to help him get some of RayVen. He didn't care if his homies got some, as long as he was first to bust that pussy open. Soon as he had her ass where he wanted her, Chains had to bring his lurking ass on the scene. That shit ain't had nothing to do with him. But he wanted to come to the bitch's rescue like he's superman or some shit. Unfortunately, one of his boys ended up bodied in the process. If Chains would have just stayed in his lane, none of that shit would have ever happened.

To make shit worse, Manolo had to spend months in solitary behind that shit, while Chains continued to receive special attention, like he was a king or some shit. By the time Manolo finally made it back to a regular cell, Chains had been released. But by then, he had his mind made up to put an end to Chains, one way or another.

"I don't give a fuck about none of that shit," he says finally. "I had to spend months in the hole while that muthafucka got luxury treatment until he walked out the front door. I couldn't think of nothing else while I was waiting on y'all to break me out. It's time to make his ass bleed."

He nods. "My sources tell me he left Jersey about a year ago. He's down in Atlanta with his wife. I think she just had a baby."

"Wife?! You mean that muthafucka married that sexy ass bitch, RayVen?" Manolo shakes his head with disgust. "Looks like I'ma be taking a trip to ATL."

"Already on the way, nephew. But we gotta play this shit cool. If you really wanna body this dude, then you gonna have to play this shit smart. With Chains being out of Jersey, he's not as untouchable as he used to be. He has two weaknesses now. And that's how we're going to break him. But you have to move how I tell you to move. You got me?"

"Don't worry Unc; I'm down with whatever you got in mind. 'Cause when all this shit is said and done, I'm gonna be known as the nigga that brought an end to Chains Verano."

As they finally hit the interstate, Manolo looks out the window with a smile on his face.

The last thing that muthafucka will see is me standing over him when I blow his fuckin' head off. Who knows, I might even drop another baby in RayVen's sexy ass when I'm done. Oh yeah, my clapback on this muthafucka is gonna be lit. But before I end him, I'm gonna take away every fucking thing he loves. Get ready for war, muthafucka.

CHAPTER 1

St. Vincent's Memorial Hospital

Atlanta, Georgia

"All right RayVen, I'm going to need you to bear down as much as possible during this next contraction."

I shake my head in disbelief. It already feels like every internal organ in my body is coming out.

"I honestly don't think I can push anymore."

Xavien leans down and kisses my damp forehead. "Baby, you got this...I'm right here with you."

I look into those green eyes of his, and the only thing that comes to mind is slapping the shit out of him. God knows I love my husband, but right now, I can't stand his punk ass. Besides, it's his fault that my ass is being ripped open by his big-headed child. If I was physically able to get out of this bed and beat his ass, I would. But in all seriousness though, this moment is surreal to me. Bringing a child into the world is a dream

I gave up on a long time ago, along with ever getting married again.

It's no secret that my first time around was the most traumatic five years of my life. My first husband was every part of an asshole that you could imagine: cruel, abusive, and cold. He cheated on me, raped me, and sometime after we divorced, he almost killed me. Because of him, I miscarried during my first pregnancy. The doctors told me that my miscarriage left me sterile, so my dreams of being a mother one day went down the drain. After enduring all those years of being abused emotionally and physically, I gave up on things that made me who I am. And when it became official that I didn't have to deal with that evil muthafucka anymore, it was safe to say that being with anyone else was the last thing on my mind.

Then in May of last year, my life was turned upside down by a prisoner named Xavien Verano aka Chains. It was just a normal day at the office, when my supervisor begged me to take on a client that my colleagues were afraid of. Shit, I'd heard the stories about him, and I was ready to run my damn self. But I put on my big girl panties and went to the prison to see what all the fuss was about. Everyone was right about him being mean as hell and one of the rudest niggas I'd ever had the displeasure of meeting. But they forgot to mention that he was finer than a muthafucka. And that's not just my biased opinion because he's my husband. In case you missed it, Xavien is half Puerto Rican, half black, 6'3", and built in all the right places. The icing on the cake is his green eyes and long, wavy hair. Trust me, when I first laid eyes on him, the last thing on my mind was anger management. But no matter how much I was lusting, he scared the shit out of me. Nonetheless, I managed to hang in there long enough to do my job. I mean, I genuinely wanted to help him create a positive change in his life. Little did I know, he would end up changing mine in the process. Xavien was by far the toughest client I've ever had; mainly because he challenged me in a way I wasn't used to. I couldn't just feed him a bunch of technical terms when he said something I didn't agree with, because he saw right through me. And he wouldn't waste any time calling me out on it. It pissed me off, but deep down, I secretly admired that about him.

But if someone had told me that his crazy ass would be my husband a year later, I would have signed them up for some type of therapy with the quickness. I didn't see our situation going past anything but our weekly sessions. But that was before the mind blowing, toe curling, screaming out in every language but English, sex he started laying on me. I swear that man did things to me I'd only read about. Long story short, I caught feelings for him. However, I got a promotion that ended up causing a falling out between us. If things weren't bad enough, my dearly departed ex—may he rest in shit—beat the hell out of me. With all the hell I'd experienced that year, taking a new job and starting over didn't seem like a bad idea. Although, I seemed to have left my heart back in Jersey. After months of not hearing from him, I eventually started to believe that I would never see Xavien Verano again. But somehow, someway, he found me and made me his.

I know we didn't meet under the most romantic circumstances, but it's been worth the craziness we endured to get to this moment. Every bad experience I've endured with my ex made me appreciate how good of a man Xavien is. He's more than I could ever ask for, and I thank God everyday for him. But like I said, the only down side is the man can see right through me.

I remember when I first missed my period in January. At the time, I was only a week late, but he didn't hesitate to ask me about it. My cycles have always been irregular, so I reassured him that it was normal for me. However, when March rolled around and I still hadn't had a period, he wasn't having it. I was making breakfast one morning and I caught him staring at me with the cutest smirk on his face.

"What?" I asked

He shrugged. "I don't know...you just looking real different today."

"Really, how so?"

He walked up to me and stroked the side of my face. "You just look so beautiful baby. Your skin is glowing and everything."

"Boy hush." I waved him off. "It's probably what you've been doing to me these past few nights."

He laughs. "Don't be tryna gas me up, girl. I think it's a little more than that, you feel me."

I turned the stove off so I can look him in the eyes. "Like what, Mr. Verano?"

He caught me off guard by rubbing my stomach. "Like maybe you're carrying my baby."

I dropped my eyes to the floor. "Xavien...I told you I can't have kids. My doctor back in Jersey was adamant about that. I'm sorry sweetie, but it's just not going to happen."

He lifted my chin with his forefinger. "Obviously, that muthafucka ain't know what he was talking about, 'cause from where I stand, it already happened. Look me in the eye and tell me that you're 100% sure you're not pregnant, and I'll drop the shit. No questions asked."

As much as I wanted to, I couldn't. I was feeling the exact same way I felt when I was pregnant with my daughter. I just didn't want to get my hopes up.

Xavien pulled me in his arms when I didn't respond. "Look Ray, I ain't claiming to be no doctor or none of that shit, but I know you. And I been around you long enough to peep when something is going on with you. Me and you go jogging every day, and you still getting thick as hell. And it ain't just from me beating that back in."

I laughed and popped him on the arm.

"Let's just go and see what's up with you real quick."

I crossed my arms defiantly in front of me. "Who says I feel like going?"

He smacked my ass. "Girl, I wasn't asking. Bring your ass on."

As you can see...that ole green eyed muthafucka was right. I grab hold of his hand as one of the worst contractions of this whole ordeal begins to take hold of me.

"Good job, RayVen...Keep pushing," the doctor tells me.

I want to tell him to go fuck himself, but I push and push, until I didn't have any strength left. Then all of sudden...I hear my baby crying. I look up and there he was.

Xavier DaeSean Verano.

And for a lack of a better word, he is perfect. Ten fingers, ten toes. Twenty-three inches long and weighing in at an even seven pounds.

We watch in silence as they clean him up and wrap him in a little blue blanket. When the nurse gently places him in my arms, I can no longer keep myself from crying. I couldn't thank God enough for blessing me with this little miracle. Xavien sits down on the bed beside me and wipes away my tears.

"Damn, he looks just like me," he says in awe.

Carefully, I place his son in his arms. There's no fighting the smile on my face as I watch the two people I love the most, meet each other for the first time. Plus, this is the only time I can recall seeing fear in Xavien's eyes.

I gently rub his arm. "You're going to be an amazing father."

He shakes his head. "I just don't want to fuck shit up for y'all, Ray."

"The only way you can do that, is if you leave us."

He leans over and kisses me. "Baby, ain't no muthafucka breathin' gonna take me away from y'all, you feel me."

I smile and rest my head on his shoulder, as I enjoy the view of our son asleep in his arms.

CHAPTER 2

Xavien

One year later...

"Mmm...this feels so amazing," RayVen moans as I massage warm oil down the length of her back.

I have her butt naked across the bed of our hotel suite, with candles lit, soft music playing, the whole nine. Thought I'd surprise my baby with something special since we've been so busy lately. With Lil' X being born and Ty moving in with us, we haven't had much one-on-one time, you feel me. I ain't gonna lie, it fucked with me just a little bit 'cause I'm used to getting it when I want it. But I ain't got no reason to trip 'cause baby girl has no problem showing me what that mouth do. I pick up the bottle of oil and pour some more over her juicy ass. RayVen's been thick since the day I met her, but carrying X made that ass phat as a muthafucka. Those pretty ass titties of hers had gone up a size or two also. She was tripping about the little bit of weight she gained during her pregnancy, but I have no problem reminding wifey that she's still sexy as fuck. I smack her ass and watch that shit jiggle

13

for me.

"Arch that shit up for me." I tell her.

She does so without a word. For a minute, I just sit back and enjoy the view of her phat pussy peeking at me from between her thick ass thighs.

"God dayum!"

I spread her legs a little wider, grab her hips, and stick my tongue in that pussy from the back.

"Ssss…Oooh Xavien," she moans.

I smother my face in that muthafucka, allowing my long ass tongue to find her spot. Those sweet juices of hers begin to drip out of her body, coating my tongue. And I gladly slurp up every drop. She starts shaking, trying her best to clench up on a nigga. You know I ain't about to let that shit happen. I let her go, only to smack both sides of that ass again.

"Turn yo' ass over."

"You're so aggressive tonight," RayVen tells me, but from the look in her eyes, I know she's loving it.

"You ain't seen shit yet."

Once she's on her back, I take hold of her calves and pull her closer. I keep my hands on the back of her thighs, keeping her legs nice and wide for me. Her thick clit is winking at me like a fat ass cherry in between her fudge-colored pussy lips. Taking my time, I allow the tip of my tongue to swirl around it. She immediately starts shaking when my tongue glides slowly down the smooth outline of where the lips meet. I kiss her clit softly before pulling it in my mouth and sucking on it.

"Ohh…my fucking…Gawd!" she screams.

RayVen arches her back, trying to run from me, but I lock my arms around her waist.

"I know you ain't trying to run from me."

She giggles. "A little bit."

"Oh, you think this a muthafuckin' game? Aight then, keep laughing."

I spread her pussy open with my fingers and drill my tongue all the way in that shit. With my arms holding her legs in place, I'm able to find her G-spot with the quickness. Her hands start gripping my hair as her body loses control.

"Aaahh…Aaahhh…. Aaahhhh!!" is the only thing I hear coming out of her mouth. I don't know why she keeps thinking I'm playin' with her ass.

I have my face so deep in that pussy, that I probably look like one of those muthafuckas in a pie eating contest or some shit. She screams my name and begins to rapidly tap my shoulder, letting me know she can't take any more. But tapping out ain't gonna save that pussy tonight. She's taking everything I got; especially this long, thick dick that's waiting on her.

"Xavien please…please no more," she begs.

I keep going until there's no doubt that I've sucked the soul out of her pussy. And it's only then that I decide to come up for air. RayVen curls up on the side of the bed, crying like she always does after she nuts too much. I give her a few minutes to get her mind right.

"You good?" I ask when she finally calms down.

She only nods.

I smack her on the hip. "Bring that ass here."

I'm chilling at the head of the bed, silently plotting on what I want to do to her next. I reach for her when she crawls towards me, but she moves out of my grip and positions herself between my legs. She leans forward and starts kissing the inside of my thigh.

"You really tryna start some shit now, ain't you?"

She gives me a sexy ass smirk before showing some attention to my other thigh. I bite my lip when I feel her soft lips travel up to my balls. She licks along the sac before taking them in her mouth.

"Ohh…fuck," I say as she sucks my shit with the right amount of pressure.

Lil' nasty ass. I've created a damn monster. I'm loving every minute of it though. Eventually, she begins jacking my dick gently while she continues to show my balls some love.

"You nasty as fuck," I tease her.

"You ain't seen shit yet," she tells me, making my dick hard as a muthafucka.

RayVen continues to stroke me with her hand and gradually brings her mouth to the head. She sucks the tip slowly, allowing her mouth to adjust to that thick muthafucka, as she takes more and more of it in her mouth. I feel the tip hit the back of her throat, and she gags, but doesn't stop. Her warm mouth fills up with spit, making that shit sound sloppy as fuck when she sucks me deep. She pulls her head back for a minute, allowing me to see the thick stream of spit trailing from my dick to her sexy ass lips. Baby girl slurps that shit up and starts putting that mouth work in overdrive. Alternating between fast and slow. Taking it deep until she gags, causing more spit to coat my dick. Then she slurps my shit dry and wets that muthafucka up again. I ain't gonna lie, she has my head gone for a minute, but I refuse to let her get the upper hand. I grab her hair with just enough force to get her mouth off me. With a hand full of her hair, I pull her to me and fuck that sloppy ass mouth with my tongue. She grabs my shoulders when I lift her hips, straddling her on my lap. I rub the head of my dick against her tight slit, causing her juices to run down my shaft.

"You gonna open up for me?" I ask, still teasing her.

"Fuck Xavien…just put it in!"

Shit, she ain't have to tell me twice. I grab a handful of that ass and bust that pussy open.

"Ohh…fuck!" RayVen screams.

She grinds her hips slowly at first, giving that shit time to adjust. Then she starts riding that shit like I taught her to.

I smack that juicy ass, egging her on. "Bounce on that muthafucka…yeah, just like that."

She leans forward so she can run her tongue over my lips. Locking my arms around her waist, I flip her onto her back. I kiss her deep then let my mouth wander from her neck to her swollen nipples. I push her titties together and suck both them muthafuckas at the same time. Her nails dig into my back when I start digging in her guts, while continuing my assault on her titties. From the way RayVen is screaming, I'm sure the people next door are gonna know my name by the time I'm done.

"Oh my god…I missed this dick!" she screams out.

I can't help laughing at her ass. Baby girl becomes a completely different person when she's getting fucked right.

"So, you don't want me to hold back on you?" I ask fucking with her.

"Please don't…I wanna feel all of you tonight."

If she keeps talking shit like this, I ain't gonna be able to hold this shit much longer. I pull out only to flip her over on her stomach. She wants to feel all of this muthafucka, then dammit she's gonna get it. I smack her ass several times and she arches up for me. Her hands grip the sheets when I slide in deep. She reaches a hand back to keep me from going any deeper, causing me to tighten my hold on her hips and snatch her closer.

"Move your fuckin' hand. You asked for this shit remember." Then I start pounding that pussy with a vengeance, reminding her who the fuck this shit belongs to.

"XAVIIEENNN…!" she cries out in a pitch I knew all too well.

I tighten my grip on her hips when her body starts to shake uncontrollably. Her hot ass pussy clamps down on me, milking every ounce of nut from my dick.

"Shiiit…baby!"

A little while later, I collapse on the bed next to her. Both of us are breathing hard as we wait for that high to come down. RayVen has this big ass smile on her face when she looks at me and shakes her head.

"What you looking at me like that for?"

"If I didn't know any better, I'd say you were trying to put another baby in me."

"Nah, just hit them walls right." I smack that ass for emphasis.

RayVen laughs. "Well, you definitely have no problem doing that, Mr. Verano." She lifts her head and looks at the clock. "Oh shoot, I forgot to call Ms. Lana and check on X. Do you think she's still up?"

I shrug. "Won't hurt to try."

A few weeks ago, Mama Armateo decided to come down and help us out with X. With him being her first grandchild and Carmine and V.J. always busy with running their father's businesses, it was a good enough reason for her to get out the house and get a change of scenery. I thought RayVen was gonna trip because she was having separation anxiety with X. But as soon as those two got around each other, it was an immediate bond.

"Anybody answer?" I ask when she put the phone back on the nightstand.

"I texted Ty and he said everyone is fine. Ms. Lana and X are asleep already."

I nod and start to yawn. "Cool. Bring dat ass back over here so I can go to sleep."

"You're so demanding." She laughs but climbs back in bed with me, laying her head on my chest.

A few minutes of silence pass then she lifts her head and kisses me on the cheek.

"What's that for?"

"For being such an amazing man to me and a wonderful father to X."

I laugh. "Not bad for a nigga who spent five years in prison for bodying muthafuckas."

"Hush…Xavien you are not that person anymore. You don't need to be. All of us are safe; we don't have any issues with money. We're fine."

I nod. "I know it's been a minute, but I did a lot of shit in my past Ray. Back then I ain't have no ties to anyone, but now I got you and X." I shake my head. "I just don't want no bullshit to come between what we got going. Shit just seems too good to be true, you feel me."

She nods. "Nothing is promised in this life, but I can guarantee that as long as you got me…I got you, no questions asked. I won't let anyone hurt you."

That was the realist shit anyone had ever said to me. And I am glad RayVen is the one to say it. I caress the side of her face as I kiss her deep. Ready to make love to her again. About an hour or so later we are both knocked out sleep.

CHAPTER 3

RayVen

*I*t's close to 7AM when I decide to get out of bed and start on breakfast. We had just gotten back from our weekend getaway the night before, and I must say, it was much needed. On the other hand, it's Monday morning and time to get back to business. Ms. Lana has been going above and beyond to help us around the house, and I wanted to give her a little break. When Xavien first suggested she come live with us for a while, I was a little skeptical. I'd only met her a few times before X was born, and she was always so sweet to me. But I am a little overprotective of my son and didn't want someone I barely know caring for him when I'm not around. But after being around her on a daily basis, I know that we all are in good hands. Although, she insists on cooking and cleaning all the time. I try to tell her she needs to relax, but she won't hear of it. But I can't complain because it's good for X to at least have a grandmother around. Although her presence is much appreciated, there isn't a day goes by where I don't wish my mother was still around to meet Xavien and X. And even though he doesn't say anything, I know Xavien feels the same. I peeked my head in her room earlier, and I'm glad to see she is sleeping peacefully. Xavien is knocked out as always, so I'm not worried about him waking up anytime soon. On the way to the kitchen, I peek into Xavier's room.

For a few moments, I just watch him sleep. I still cannot believe that God blessed us with something so beautiful. Look at him with his little chunky self. Honey brown skin, thick wavy hair, and green eyes like his dad. The only thing he inherited from me so far is his dimples, but other than that, you would think his father spit him out. I'm already dreading the day when he gets older and he has little girls coming around looking for him. If he's anything like his dad, Lord help us. Gently, I run my hands through his soft hair before heading downstairs. Although I almost trip over a toy truck on the way to the kitchen, I manage to make it there without turning on any lights. I never realized how much I took a peaceful house for granted until I had to share it with a family.

I'd barely started cooking when I hear the alarm chirp and the side door creeping open then shut. I turn around to see Ty trying to sneak past me to his room.

"Ahem!" I say loud enough to get his attention.

"Good morning, Ma," he says casually, like he didn't have class in a few hours.

"Don't *good morning*, Ma' me. Where have you been all night, knowing you have class today?"

He gets this little slick ass grin on his face. "I told X I was going out to get my wig twisted."

"Mm hmm…keep playing with me."

After doing some investigating on Ty's foster parents, I discovered they were mistreating him. I couldn't stand to see him being bounced around somewhere else, so Xavien and I took custody of him. It works out well because we have more than enough space. And I can sleep better at night knowing he's safe. Since he's been with us, he hasn't been fighting as much, and he's been doing well in school. Plus, he needs a strong male role model in his life who has been on both sides of the track. Trust me, it hasn't been all sunshine and roses between those two; especially, when tempers get to flaring. I swear sometimes it feels like I'm watching Xavien argue with a younger version of himself. They are just that similar. I've had to settle plenty of arguments over this past year. But I thank God, they've been able to work out an understanding. I know Ty is just afraid of things not working out. When you add that to him just turning 17 and going through all these hormonal changes, I can kind of understand his mood swings. But he's never gotten so out of line that I've regretted our decision. It's crazy how much he's grown up in this short amount of time. Seems like only yesterday he was the stubborn kid getting into fights in the cafeteria.

He removes the hood off his head to show me his fresh braids. "See, I wouldn't lie to you."

"I know it doesn't take all night to do cornrows."

He drops his hazel eyes to the floor.

"Listen, I trust you and you know we don't mind if you go out, but at least let me know so I won't worry about you. It's too much mess going on in these streets nowadays." I touch the side of his face. "I know I'm not your mother, but I just don't want anything happening to you, Ty."

I turn my attention back to the stove to make sure the food isn't burning. Ty catches me off guard by wrapping his long arms around my shoulders.

"I'm sorry to make you worry," he tells me. "You and X have looked out for me more than anybody, and I would never do y'all dirty. And I don't care what anyone says, you are my mama."

I hug him back and the faint smell of perfume hits my nose. "I hear you...just be careful with that little female you are sneaking around with."

"Huh?"

"Huh...my ass. The only baby I want to deal with right now is Xavier."

"I can't tell from the way you and X be smashing," he mumbles slyly

I chop him with a plastic spatula across the shoulder and he starts laughing. "Boy, I heard that. Don't play with me."

"Nigga, don't be huggin' on my wife like that," Xavien says as he walks into the kitchen.

Ty hugs me again and sticks his middle finger up. "This my mama nigga."

"Get fucked up."

I can only shake my head as the two them start laughing and bump fists.

"Yo X, I'm gonna need to holla at you about that situation I asked you about."

Xavien nods. "Aight, catch me in a few."

"Wait, y'all can't talk in front of me?" I ask.

Ty starts laughing and takes off upstairs.

"Xavien, what was that all about?"

He walks up behind me and wraps his arms around my waist. My knees get weak when he starts kissing my neck.

"Are you avoiding my question?"

"Stop being so damn nosey."

I suck my teeth and push him off me, faking an attitude. "Fine then."

Xavien catches me off guard by turning me around and picking me up until we are eye-to-eye.

"I know you ain't got no attitude with me."

I roll my eyes at him. "Put me down. I have to finish breakfast."

He continues to hold me up with one hand while stirring the food with the other. "Do I gotta remind you what the fuck my name is?" There is a look in his eyes that I haven't seen since the first time we met.

I stick my tongue out causing him to laugh. He kisses me and puts me back on my feet. "X is still knocked out, so we should be cool for a minute."

I nod. "That will give me just enough time to get breakfast finished and take a shower."

"Aight, if he wakes up before then I'll get him straight." He smacks me on the ass. "Lemme know when the food is ready, big booty."

I laugh and playfully push him on the shoulder.

*****

"X, do we have to go through this every morning?" I ask my one-year-old.

We had gotten through having a nice family breakfast, getting him dressed, and made it through this crazy ass traffic without him showing his behind. But it seems every morning when he has to go to daycare he has to throw a fit because he doesn't want me to leave.

He starts screaming at the top of his lungs in response to my question.

"Fine, you can stand here with this mess. I'm going to work." I turn around and pretend like I'm walking away from him.

"Mommy, don't go!" He runs behind me and grabs hold of my leg.

I stoop down so I can look him in the eye. "Are you done misbehaving?"

He nods his head.

"Here, clean your face man." He takes the tissue from my hand and wipes his face like I taught him to. "Ok, I want you to be a big boy and go to school, ok."

He nods. "Okay."

"Are you going to draw me a picture?"

He smiles then, showing me his adorable dimples. "Yes Mommy."

"Ok, let's go."

X holds my hand as I walk him back to the classroom to his teacher. He takes her hand, following her inside.

I watch him turn around to wave goodbye to me. "I love you, Mommy."

"I love you too, sweetie." With tears in my eyes, I watch him get settled in at one of the tiny desks and begin to draw with one of the crayons.

Lord, I don't want to leave my baby. I take a deep breath and dry my eyes before heading down the hall to the other building.

When I found out I was pregnant, I suggested to Mr. Mitchell that we open one of the empty classrooms at Epic and turn it into a daycare center. When I thought about how hard it's going to be working 8-10 hours a day, on top of running a household, then adding the stress of having to worry about fighting through traffic to pick my baby up on time from daycare, I knew I had to do something that will not only benefit me, but my coworkers as well. Every woman doesn't have a reliable man at home willing to help her out with raising a child. So, opening this daycare seemed like the best option to help the ladies who are struggling with childcare and working full-time. I've heard so many horror stories about kids being abused at daycare centers. And there isn't a jury in the world that will convict me if someone lays a hand on my son. And ensuring the safety of my baby and every other baby in this center is a must. Of course, when the corporate office heard about my idea they stipulated charging a fee if they were going to give their approval on the daycare service. I guess it's too much of an inconvenience for them to invest in something that would actually be beneficial to their employees. Especially, without them making a profit. But I wasn't having it. With the help of my father, I was able to invest in the service myself to make it happen. And I'm pleased to say, everything has been going well with it so far.

Anyway, when I finally make it to my office, I'm caught off guard by the bouquet of lilies sitting on my desk. It had been a minute since Xavien sent me flowers, but when he does, he always sends pink and white roses. There's a small envelope with my name on it lying next to the vase. An uneasy feeling settles in my stomach when I open the envelope and read the card.

Lilies are white, Violets are blue

You don't know me yet, but

You're definitely about to.

Signed,

Your Secret Admirer ;-)

"What the fuck?" I say to myself as I continue to read the card over and over.

And just like a scene out of a horror movie, the phone in my office begins to ring. I take a deep breath and pick up the receiver.

"Good morning, it's a wonderful day at Epic Changes." There's dead silence on the other end for like 30 seconds. "Hello, you've reached Epic Changes," I repeat.

"Damn, I knew you had a sexy ass voice," an accented male voice says finally.

"Who is this?" I ask.

"Did you get the flowers I sent you? I know your man sends you roses all the time, so I know I had to come at you different."

My heart is racing a mile a minute, but I try to keep calm. "How do you know my husband?"

He chuckles a little. "I know a lot."

I'm not going to lie, this dude has me shook. But I attempt to brush it off. It has to be one of the kids at the center playing a joke or something.

"Listen, if this is your idea of a joke, you can take that shit somewhere else. Goodbye."

"Those white pants you got on got your ass looking real phat... mmm...and I'm loving that tight ass blue shirt too. Got your titties looking right," he says. "Almost made me jack my dick while looking at you."

"Fuck you, all right!"

"Soon baby, real soon. Enjoy the rest of your day...RayVen."

The phone goes dead, and I stand there for almost five minutes listening to the dial tone. I replay his voice in my head, trying to see if it matched anyone at the center. And I draw a blank. He doesn't sound like any of the kids here. The only thing I do know is he's Hispanic or something. With trembling hands, I finally hang up the receiver. As soon as I think my day is going well, some nutcase has to call me with this nonsense. But it was only one phone call, so I shrug it off for now. I throw the flowers in a nearby trash can and make a quick trip to the daycare center to check on my baby.

CHAPTER 4

Xavien

"*X*, I'm telling you dude, ole girl was all over me last night, like she couldn't wait to get some of me."

I shake my head at Ty as he fills me in on his latest smash session. Can't tell lil' homie he ain't a playa. RayVen wants me to give him advice, hoping to keep him from messing with the wrong female. But I started fucking when I was a little younger than him, so the only advice I can give him is to wrap his shit up. You can talk all day, but a hard-headed young dude is gonna do what he wants regardless. Trust me, I know.

"You smash raw?" I ask him.

"Hell nah, I heard some shit about her, so I just let her gimme that sloppy you know. It wasn't all that, but I nutted and that's all that matters. I got this other female I'm supposed to be hooking up with later; she's a little older, but I'm up for the challenge."

I laugh with him. Dude sounds just like me at that age.

"You been with a lot of females before you got with RayVen, right?"

he asks outta nowhere.

I look at the lil' nigga sideways. "What, you on some snitch shit now, fam?"

He laughs. "Nah, I just wondered what made you settle for one."

I nod. "On some real shit, she was different from what I was used to. I know you hear females feed you that bullshit about how different they are from the rest. But they end up doing the same shit as the last. Trust me, I been with every kinda female you can think of. I could be out solo with X and they still try to get at me. But I know what I got at home and ain't shit worth fuckin' that up."

He nods. "RayVen must be got that A1."

"She do," I admit, causing him to laugh. "But before we even got to that point she went out of her way to show me she fucks with a nigga. Back then I was just some dude she was tryna help get outta prison. I gave her a hard time 'cause I thought she was full of shit, but…she proved me wrong."

"I believe that. Back when she first started at the center, I used to act real salty towards RayVen. I was like, here we go, somebody else coming with that fake shit. But one day they was about to throw me in lock up and she stood up for me. I couldn't figure out why she would do that when she didn't even know me. After everything went down, she took me to get something to eat and everything. At first I thought she was doing it to get on my good side, but I finally realized she was just cool like that. And if I was gonna fuck with anybody back at the center, it was gonna be her."

"Yeah, she's a real one."

32

He nods again. "That's why I see her as my mom, 'cause even though she ain't have me, she don't treat me no different than X."

"I feel you on that shit," I tell him, thinking back to how Mama Armateo accepted me with open arms to help my mom keep an eye on me.

A few minutes later, we pull up to this new site we recently got a contract for. I never would've thought my construction business would blow up the way it has. When I first started out, I just wanted to put dudes on who were looking for a second chance. Word spread fast and before I knew it, there was a bunch of dudes hitting me up for a job. After doing a background check on everybody who came through, I ended up with almost 30 new employees working for me. With more hands available, we can get more done, so it doesn't take us long to get a building up and running. That comes in real handy for muthafuckas who want their shit done in a hurry, and they have no problem coming out of pocket for quality service. So far, I ain't have to worry about nobody complaining about working too much or not getting enough hours or any of that other bullshit. Anyway, this new site is some kinda office building that the city wanted opened within the next few weeks. They were having some electrical and plumbing problems, and they wanted us to check it out.

As I drive further onto the site, I see a box Chevy already in the parking lot, which meant Ty's homies from the center, Kyle and Mike, were already inside. I look around and none of the other dudes have made it to the site yet.

"X. I'm about to go ahead and help those dudes out," he says, jumping out the car and grabbing his gear.

"Aight, I'll be out in a minute."

I had barely stuck my key in the office door when the phone starts ringing.

"This Verano," I say when I finally make it in to pick up the receiver.

All I hear is somebody breathing on the other end, so I hang up the phone. I don't have time for the dumb shit. Stupid ass muthafucka. After I grab what I need, I'm ready to head out and get started. That is, until I hear a loud ass explosion that shakes the whole office. The shit was so strong I would've sworn it was a damn earthquake or something. Without a second thought, I take off outside towards the building. The air is filled with this thick ass cloud of black smoke, as it seeps from the broken glass of the window, making it hard to breathe. My heart is racing like a muthafucka as I call for Ty and the two other dudes. The sound of someone coughing on the other side of the building causes me to haul ass in that direction. I see Ty and Kyle dragging their friend Mike out one of the side doors. From the looks of things he doesn't seem to be breathing. I scoop dude up over my shoulder and carry him away from the building.

I don't know who called the fire department, but it was appreciated. I'm glad it doesn't take all fucking day for them to get here with the paramedics. They spend the first few minutes checking on Mike before making sure the rest of us are straight. He's banged up really bad from the blast, but they say he should pull through all right. After the smoke is cleared, some dude pulls up in a black Expedition.

He must be somebody with some pull 'cause I saw him exchange a few words with the police before walking towards me.

"Mr. Verano, I apologize for this mishap. I didn't know the wiring in this building was that bad."

"And you are?"

"Marciano Barajas, this is my building that you were commissioned to work on."

I only nod.

"Is the young man going to be ok? The officers told me someone was injured."

"He'll be cool. I gotta make sure my people get home safe."

I leave dude and his tailored suit at the site while I get my shit and roll. Kyle is too shaken up to drive, so I drop him off at his crib before taking Ty home. Mama Armateo lost her mind when she saw the bruises on Ty, and I had no choice but to tell her what happened. After getting cleaned up, she insisted we eat and rest. But after what just happened, there was no way I was sleeping. So, I hop in my ride and make my way to RayVen's job. I ain't gonna lie that shit had me fucked up. If Ty and his friends had been deeper into the building, they would have been taken out. Shit, I could have easily gotten fucked up. I just needed to see my wife right now. When I got in the building, I noticed Ms. Agnes, the usual receptionist, wasn't there. She was an older lady with thick glasses. In her own way, she was cool 'cause she always wanted to buy stuff for X. But today, there is this Latin female sitting in her spot. She seems to be about our age, if not a few years younger. She looks like she was dressed to go to the club with her titties hanging out and the short ass skirt she had on. I guess that's why they have her up front instead of around the kids.

"Welcome to Epic Changes. My name is Marianna may I help you, Sir," she says, licking her lips and smiling at me.

"I'm here to see, RayVen Verano," I tell her.

"Oh, are you a friend or relative of RayVen's?"

Is this chick retarded or something? "Nah, I'm her husband."

That still doesn't stop her from smiling up in my face. "Well your…um wife is in her office. If you need anything, and I do mean anything, give me a call." She winks at me.

I don't even bother responding to this dizzy bitch as I make my way to RayVen's office. She tells me to come in after I knock.

"Hey!" RayVen jumps up and wraps her arms around me. "I wasn't expecting you so soon."

It felt so good to have her in my arms. For a long time I just hold her tightly, enjoying the feel of her next to me.

"Xavien, what's wrong?" she asks when she notices I didn't say anything.

I finally let her go. "There was an explosion at the site today. One of the boys got hurt."

"Oh my god! Are you ok?" She takes my face in her hands and kisses me several times. "How's Ty?"

"He's cool, just shaken up a little."

She nods. "I'll cancel the rest of my clients for today so I can make sure all of you are ok."

"Nah, we'll be cool. Ain't no need for both of us to miss work," I tell her. "I just needed to lay eyes on you. And I can take X home early so you don't have to stress about that."

She sighs and touches the side of my face. "You sure, boo?"

I nod.

"Okay, you want to wait for me in the hall while I go get X?"

"Nah, I can get him."

"Baby, you've been through enough today. Just relax."

So now I'm sitting in the hallway with this thirsty bitch, Marianna, staring at me. I start playing a game on my phone so she won't think I'm trying to give her any time.

"You know, you look just like this dude I knew back in Jersey. He was fine and had some sexy ass green eyes just like you. But he was a street dude though; hardcore, a real savage ass nigga. Not soft like you seem to be."

I was already on edge from earlier so I wasn't about to sit here and deal with this bullshit. "Bitch, ain't shit soft over here. Better watch who the fuck you pop off to, you feel me."

That slick ass smile of her seems to get wider. "I knew it was you; been a long time Chains."

I shake my head. This was one of those days I really wish RayVen would hurry the fuck up. 'Cause I definitely didn't have time for this shit. Somebody must have answered my prayers 'cause a few minutes later, she came around the corner with X sleeping on her shoulder. I take him out of her hands, trying my best not to wake him. When

RayVen hands me his bag, I lean down and stick my tongue in her throat. Putting that bitch on notice that I already have a woman.

"See you at home, baby."

"You ok?" she asks with a smile.

There's no hiding the pissed off expression on Marianna's face. I smile and give my baby a kiss on the forehead.

"Now I am."

With X in tow, I head out the door to my ride. During the drive home, I try to backtrack in my memory how deep things went with Marianna. Her name does sound familiar, but I doubt I ever smashed. So it must not have been that serious. Whatever the case may be, she still seems kinda hung up on a nigga. And from how scandalous she was acting at RayVen's job, I can tell she's not above starting shit. I just hope and pray my past doesn't come back to haunt me. But I have no problem burying any muthafucka who fucks with me or my family. I take a quick glance at X, who's still knocked out, and continue on down the road.

CHAPTER 5

$\mathcal{I}$ stand in the doorway of the center until I can no longer see the tail lights of Xavien's car. *God, please watch over my babies and allow them to make it home safe. Amen.* When I head back inside, I notice the receptionist, Mariana, or whatever the hell her name is, rolling her eyes at me. In the short time I've been at Epic, it's safe to say I have never had any issues with anyone. Mr. Mitchell had done an excellent job of establishing teamwork between the employees. It doesn't matter if you are a receptionist, custodian, or therapist, at the end of the day all of us are here to do a job. The best thing is no one is treated any more importantly than anyone else, and we all pitch in to help one another. More importantly, there was never any drama. That is, until about two months ago when Ms. Agnes had to go out for a hip replacement.

She is by far one of the sweetest women I have ever met. I mean she would go above and beyond to help you if she was able to. Ms. Agnes played a big part in helping me get adjusted when I first started here. And she was the only one who could get me to stay off my feet during my pregnancy. After Ms. Agnes went out on leave, there have been two other receptionists who have tried to fill her shoes. I thought they were working out well, but they seemed to have left as quickly as they come. Anyway, ever since Marianna started, I noticed a subtle shift in our peaceful work atmosphere. As soon as she walked into the building, it was like a dark cloud hovering over us. I mean, the air of arrogance surrounding this woman is just that thick. Like she was doing us a favor by working here. Homegirl walked in here with a miniskirt, stiletto heels, and her shirt unbuttoned almost to the navel. I know I can't tell a grown ass individual how to dress, but as adults with troubled children, none of us should want to be a negative influence. The last thing I want is the young men to have a negative view on what makes women attractive. And I definitely don't want the girls to feel like they have to expose themselves to be of value. The media does enough of that already without us adding to the bullshit. Nevertheless, it's always customary when we get a new member on our team to give them a warm welcome and introduce ourselves.

The only time she seemed interested is when Mr. Mitchell spoke and when I introduced myself to her. The whole time I spoke she kind of smirked at me like she was aware of something I wasn't. I try to give everyone the benefit of the doubt, but something about this chick doesn't sit right with me. Ever since that day there have been some confrontations between her and a few of my coworkers. Thank God, none of them have turned physical, but there have been a few close calls. If you were to look up the word thot in the dictionary, you would see a picture of Marianna with her legs open. Not only is the bitch reckless with her mouth, but she can't seem to stay away from other men who are attached. I remember one afternoon when I had to keep my coworker Tanya for stomping a mudhole in the bitch.

On that particular day, Tanya and I were on our way back from checking on the kids at daycare, and we wanted to go on our lunch break a little early. Anyway, Tanya's boyfriend was kind enough to pick up lunch for us and bring it by. So, we're on our way to the lobby and Marianna is taking the food out of his hand. She was so close to him that I thought she was trying to put her titties in the man's mouth.

"What the fuck is going on here?" Tanya asks as she storms over to them.

Marianna smirked at her. She clearly thought the shit was funny. "Oh, I was just going to tip the delivery man."

"Bitch, that's no delivery man, and I suggest you keep your fucking hands to yourself."

"Well, he didn't seem to have a problem with it. Did you boo?"

It took the both of us to keep Tanya from snatching Marianna's head from her shoulders. To be quite honest, the only reason I stopped her is because I didn't want Tanya to lose her job for fighting in the workplace. Since that day, I've heard countless rumors of similar events taking place with Marianna. Recently, I noticed she's been staying late to have private meetings with Mr. Mitchell. He seemed like a sensible man thus far, so I hope he isn't stupid enough to listen to the head between his legs instead of the one on his shoulders.

At any rate, I decided the best thing for me to do is keep my distance. Now my plan was to go back to my office without even acknowledging her. That is, until that bitch sucks her teeth and mumbles something under her breath.

"I'm sorry, do you have a problem?" I ask her.

She gets that cocky smirk on her face again. "I was just saying it was good to see my old friend Chains again. I didn't figure him for the type to have a baby mama. Guess people do change over time."

"Sweetheart, I'm nobody's baby mama." I hold up my left hand. "In case someone forgot to inform you, this ring on my finger means he's my husband, and that baby that you saw him leave with is our son. So, I suggest you remember that the next time you see him."

She rolls her eyes at me. "Whatever, I've heard plenty of females run that game before. Those same "husbands" that claim to be married are hitting me up when their lame ass wives can't satisfy them in bed. So, I'd be careful with a man that fine, lame."

I step to her, putting this bitch on notice that I'm not playing with her. And I'm definitely not afraid of her. "Understand this here, because you clearly got me fucked up. I don't give two fucks about losing this job. If you fuck with me or my family, I will spare no expense in drawing blood from your ass. Now I dare you to try me, bitch."

Marianna only glares at me and I stare her ass down, refusing to back down from her.

"Everything ok here, ladies?" Mr. Mitchell asks out of nowhere.

"Fine," I tell him, my eyes still burning a hole through Marianna.

"RayVen, when you're ready we'd like to start our meeting."

I gradually back away from Marianna and follow Mr. Mitchell to the conference room. On the way, he keeps asking if I am ok. I assure him that I'm fine, but I guess the expression on my face said otherwise. Since being with Xavien, I'd changed a lot and most of it has been for the better. I will never forget the night Jaylen beat my ass and almost killed me. If Xavien hadn't shown up when he did, I probably wouldn't be here. The more I thought about it, the more I got tired of being the damsel in distress who was always waiting for her knight in shining armor to save her. I went to Xavien and asked him to teach me how to defend myself. If anyone can show me how to stomp a mudhole in someone's ass, I know my husband can. After explaining to him how I felt, he was more than happy to show me how to become official with my hands, as he calls it. When there was no doubt I could handle myself, he called his brothers and they taught me some other things. V.J. is a weapons expert so he taught me how to shoot a gun. It was a little overwhelming at first, but I eventually got the hang of it. Once I was good enough, he gave me a gun of my own to keep with me at all times, as well as some brass knuckles. Carmine studies Taekwondo in his spare time, so of course I asked him to show me some of his moves. Xavien has been cool about letting me practice on him. Every time they come down we have a little sparring match, and I've impressed them on several occasions. I don't brag about my extracurricular activities, so I wish that bitch would try me.

When I finally calm down, I wish I could say that my mind has shifted back to business. But that would be a lie. The comment she made about Xavien being an old friend of hers didn't sit well with me at all. I know he had a different life long before he met me and I can't fault him for his past. But just the thought of him fucking someone like her is enough to make my skin crawl. Before we got married, he

43

sat me down and told me everything in his past that he may not have mentioned before. I hated to hear all that, but I love and respect him enough to not hold it against him. And I don't know of too many men who would be so upfront with their women. Up until now, it hasn't really been an issue.

About an hour or so later, Mr. Mitchell is done briefing us on everything that is going on with the corporate office and how it will affect the center. I stay a little later to make sure the kids on my assignment have made it safely to their foster parents, or have an assigned bed for the night. By the time I make it back to the main office, it's nearly dark. I text Xavien real quick to let him know that I'm on my way home. As I'm turning the key to lock my office, I hear commotion coming from down the hall. The only office in that direction belongs to Mr. Mitchell. Since I don't see anyone else around, I decide to go to check on him. The last thing I want to have on my conscious is the man dying when I was here to save his life. After I've traveled a few steps, the moans coming from his office become more noticeable. I'm not sure if they don't know or they don't care, but the door to the office is open. All I see is Marianna bent over his desk with her skirt hiked up over her hips. His eyes are clenched shut while he fucks her from behind.

"You like this pussy don't you, Tim?" she asks him.

"Yes, of course…" He grabs her nipples and squeezes them while continuing to dig deeper into her hips. "But we can't keep doing this, Marianna."

She pushes him off her and drops down to her knees to take his dick in her mouth. "I'll just have to change your mind then, won't I?"

Seeing him with his eyes rolled up in his head while she sucks him off is enough to make me sick. To make matters worse, he was fucking the bitch raw. See what I get for trying to be helpful. Believe me, if I hear anything unsettling in the future, he and everyone else is on their own. I only shake my head in disgust and run out the building to my car. I can't believe he would compromise his position at the center for an office fling. Hold up, I know I can't talk because shit happens. But at least when I first fucked Xavien it was at his house, but that was a whole different story.

For some reason, I start to think about the phone call I received earlier. I don't know if it's because it is dark outside or old memories haunting me, but I get an uneasy feeling as I walk through the parking lot. Had someone really been watching me earlier? Is someone watching me now? A cold shiver runs down my spine as I think about the possibility of some nutcase nearby watching my every move. I waste no time hitting the unlock button on my keychain and jumping into my car. Once the doors are locked and I make certain no one is inside with me, I begin to relax. That is, until I see a single white lily resting on my windshield wipers. I wasn't going to be like the dumb bitch in the movies who gets out of her car and tries to remove it. So I haul ass out of the parking lot.

During the drive home, I try to think of a way to tell Xavien about what happened today without upsetting him. One of the many things I loved about him is all I have to do is call, and he'll be by my side no questions asked. But I can tell he is already on edge from the explosion at his job site earlier. And I see no reason to upset him any more than he already is. Hopefully, this is just a one-time thing. I'm sure whoever it is has more than likely gotten this out of their system by now and moved on. Thirty agonizing minutes later, I've safely made it home to my family. Of course, as I'm on my way in, Ty is on his way out.

"Ty, really?" I ask with an annoyed look on my face.

He smirks at me. "What? All my school work is done."

I shake my head at him. "I better not hear about you falling asleep in class."

"You won't and I promise I'll be careful."

I hit him on the behind with my purse. "You better be."

It doesn't take a rocket scientist to figure out he's sexually active. All these late-night escapades and top-secret conversations with Xavien. Not to mention the Magnum that fell out of his pocket when I was doing laundry one day. The only reason I threw it away is because I didn't want X finding it and thinking it was candy. Imagine trying to explain to a doctor how your baby swallowed a condom. That's a conversation I definitely didn't want to have. A part of me was concerned at first when I found out about Ty's extracurricular activities. He and Xavien thought they were too slick for me to figure out what they were talking about. But I caught the tail end of their conversations a time or two. With Ty getting sex tips from my husband, I just feel sorry for the poor girls he's dealing with. But like any concerned parent, I don't want him to get caught up in anything that can potentially ruin his life. These young girls today will do anything to try to trap a man. It's sad there are so many teenagers out here dealing with baby mama drama instead of worrying about going to college. I know I can't stop Ty from doing what he's doing. But at least I can breathe a little easier knowing he's smart enough to use protection.

During the drive home, my mind was focused solely on taking a shower and going to sleep, but the most delicious smell draws me towards the kitchen. I follow it to find Ms. Lana fixing a plate of food. She smiles as soon as she sees me.

"I heard you coming in, so I warmed you up a little something to eat," she tells me.

"Ms. Lana, you didn't have to do that." I take the plate of food and have a seat at the table.

She waves me on. "My dear, I know what it's like to run a household full of hard-headed men. They will make you lose your mind if you let them."

I laugh and take a bite of the pasta primavera and garlic bread she prepared. My eyes close as it melts in my mouth.

"And I just wanted to thank you for allowing me to share this time with you. I know I'm no replacement for the loss of your mother, but giving me the opportunity to spend time with my grandson brings a joy to my heart I haven't felt since losing Vincenzo."

Finally, I understand why she fusses over us so much. And my heart aches for her. It's been almost two years since Mr. Armateo passed and I couldn't imagine the pain she was feeling. To have spent all those years loving someone, building a family with them, and creating a lifetime of memories, just to lose him so suddenly. I was tripping about losing Xavien after only being married two years. So I know it has to be tough on her after all the years they've been together.

"How long were the two of you together?"

She fixes herself a cup of tea and takes a seat next to me. "Almost 40 years; we were married for 32."

I shake my head. "Wow, people don't stay married for that long these days."

She nods in agreement. "Marriage is hard work. Young people today don't want to put the time and effort in to keep the marriage strong. Nowadays it's all for show. Back when I was young, you rarely heard of divorce. It was thought of as a shameful thing. So women had to go through a lot to make their marriages last."

"Can you give me any advice to help with my marriage?"

She stares at me for a moment. "Are things not going well with you and Xavien?"

"No, no things have been great so far…" I sigh heavily as I prepare to open up about my concerns. "There's this woman at my job who says she used to know Xavien way back when, and she was trying to flirt with him earlier."

"Did he respond to her?"

"No ma'am, not from what I can tell." I sigh again. "I know Xavien is used to having a lot of women and seeing this female has me worried that one day I won't be enough."

She nods knowingly. "I know that feeling all too well, my dear. Vincenzo was a very powerful man, even in his younger days. And there wasn't a woman in New Jersey who didn't want the title as his wife. I know I wasn't his first choice, but I made him realize that I was a diamond in a world full of rhinestones. And he couldn't find better than me."

I laugh. "How'd you do that?"

"By praying for him, supporting him, always listening to him, and encouraging him. And when that didn't work, I put my foot in his ass."

We share a laugh.

"Xavien has his ways, I know, but he is a good man. His mother did an amazing job with him, and when she couldn't get through to him, I did. So, continue to do what you've been doing. You're his diamond. He's not going to find anyone more special than you."

I hug her then. "Thank you so much, Ms. Lana."

"You're welcome, my dear. There's plenty in the pot so don't be shy."

A wave of relief sweeps over me after my conversation with Ms. Lana. I hate to admit I was feeling a bit insecure about myself. I know I'd gained some weight since my pregnancy. I'm not huge or anything like that; I just have more booty and boobs than I'm used to. Believe me, I'm not complaining about my extra curves, but I've seen the type of women Xavien used to deal with. And they don't look anything like me. I don't know, maybe it's just those old insecurities of mine creeping up on me again. Jaylen has been dead and gone for over a year, but sometimes the abuse I suffered from him feels like yesterday. Sometimes I can still taste the blood in my mouth from when he punched me. Or how low he made me feel when he would put me down because I wasn't a size two. One incident comes to mind when we were going through our divorce. He was pissed because I wouldn't lend him any money to pay off his debts. And when begging didn't work, he resorted to insults.

You know what RayVen, he said, I'm so glad we're getting divorced. The only reason I married you is because I felt sorry for you, and your mother practically begged me to go out with you. That's why I cheated on you so much. You are fat and disgusting. Every time I fucked you I was thinking about someone else. When this bullshit is over, I'll have a real woman to come home to at night. Get used to being alone, because you will never find anyone better than me.

I'm not going to lie, that shit was a low blow, and it hurt for a minute. But that was the type of shit he would say. For five years I dealt with that type of abuse. I spent so much time pretending to be ok and helping other people, but on the inside, I was slowly dying. Now that I'm with Xavien, I'm actually happy, but it seems like all the stuff I kept buried is coming to the surface. I hate that I worry about if he's going to cheat on me. Or if he gets mad enough one day will he hit me? Xavien is a lot stronger than Jaylen, and I know if he ever puts his hands on me, the damage may be irreversible. So far, things with us have been perfect, for a lack of a better word. But now I know what Xavien meant last week when he said things feel too good to be true.

CHAPTER 6

Xavien

While RayVen is in the shower, I go through the house real quick to make sure everything is locked up. Of course, Mama Armateo fell asleep with the TV on again. And I can only shake my head. I love her to death, but I ain't tryna pay no high ass light bill. I'm able to turn it off without waking her up though. Ty is still out; probably banging somebody daughter back in. So, I ain't too worried about him. Besides, he gotta key and is able to handle himself if something goes down. Just hope the lil' nigga is strapping up like he claims he is. On the way back up to the room, I hear X making noise in his room, causing me to go down the hall to see what his problem is. When I walk in, he's standing up in the crib holding onto the rails. He starts smiling as soon as he sees me. I'm still trippin' over having a son. It wasn't too long ago when I said this shit was never gonna happen. But I guess you can never say never. And looking at him, I have no regrets about him being mine.

"Daddy!" He starts bouncing up and down like I'm about to be up all night playing with him.

I stoop down in front of the crib until we are eye-to-eye. "You know you supposed to be sleep, right?"

He smiles at me.

"Ain't nobody laughing with you dude, it's almost ten o'clock."

X holds up his hands and I pick him up to check his draws.

"You gotta pee?"

He nods.

I take him into the bathroom and sit him on the toilet. He sits there for a little while swinging his short ass legs and babbling.

"X, quit playing with me."

Two seconds later, he starts peeing. I clean his little ass and get him situated to go back to sleep.

"Aight, take your little behind to sleep," I tell him. "If I gotta come back in here we gonna have it out, you feel me."

He hugs me and I kiss him on the forehead before laying him back in the crib. I wait a few minutes until I hear him snoring lightly, then I'm able to creep back to my room. After X came into the world, it ain't take long for us to realize we had to learn how to move when he falls asleep. Lately though, he's been good about sleeping through the night, so I ain't complaining. Too many times I've heard dudes bitchin' about never getting no time in with they ole lady cause of kids. I ain't gone lie, it was rough at first, but eventually we were able to get him on our schedule. A lot of dudes are surprised that I help RayVen out so much when it comes to X. But I'm like, muthafucka she ain't got pregnant by herself. I was the one up in them guts damn near every night. And hell no I didn't pull out. So since we both went half on X,

I'm gonna do what the fuck I gotta do to help raise him. Both of us are working full-time but our son ain't lacking for nothing. Whatever my wife needs help with, I got her, no questions asked. When X grows up, he's gonna know who the fuck his father is and that I always had his back. And I'm gonna definitely make sure he knows that I always did right by his mama. So he'll know how to treat a female when he meets the right one. Shit, I ain't raising no fuck nigga. So, fuck all that extra shit.

When I finally get back to our room, I see RayVen standing in the mirror looking at her reflection. She has on this nice little negligee I bought her a few months back for Valentine's Day. Look at her ova there looking like a muthafuckin' snack. Damn, my baby is one sexy ass woman! It's crazy how she's still able to blow my mind after all this time. The pink color of the lingerie stands out against her deep chocolate skin. I watch as she runs her hands down the length of her body, inspecting her curves. The straps look like they're struggling to keep her massive titties from spilling out the top. I follow her hands with my eyes as she pulls the fabric away from her pudgy abdomen and smooths the material down over her wide hips.

Here she goes with that bullshit again. I shake my head. Walking up behind her, I wrap my arms tightly around her soft waist. She sighs when I kiss her neck several times.

"What the fuck is you doing?"

She drops her eyes to the floor when she realizes I'm looking at her reflection trying to study her face. "Nothing."

RayVen tries to move, but I keep her in front of the mirror. "Look at yourself," I tell her. Gently, I lift her chin with my fingers when she refuses to raise her head. "You can't see how fine you are if you always staring at your feet."

She shakes her head. "I'm not…"

"Yes, the fuck you are." I take a minute and run my hands down her sexy ass body. "Look at you, baby. Look at them pretty ass brown eyes. I know people would pay money for these sexy ass lips. You're fuckin' gorgeous. I hit the jackpot when I met your ass."

She starts blushing. "Shut up."

"Nah, you started this shit." I twirl her around in front me. "Mmm…mmm…mmm sexy as fuck. Ole thick, juicy ass." I grab her ass with both hands. "This my shit, you feel me. You better not ever give my pussy away. I'll go to war for your ass, girl." I start nibbling on her neck.

"Stop!" RayVen laughs.

"There's that pretty ass smile. Come here lemme holla at you." I pull her over to the bed and sit her on my knee. "Tell Daddy what's going on with you."

"Just feeling a little self-conscious."

I shake my head. "I don't see why you always doubting yourself like that. Ain't shit wrong with you, baby. Just 'cause you've gotten a little thicker, that don't change how I feel about you. You will always be the most beautiful woman in the world to me. And I'm proud to have you as my wife."

She brushes away a few tears that were creeping down her cheeks.

"You really mean that?"

I stick my tongue in her mouth, kissing her long and deep. "What you think?"

I pick her up in my arms, carrying her to bed. After putting the cover over us, I pull her in my arms and let her rest her head on my chest. My hands rub her back, stopping only to squeeze her ass every so often. Being this close to RayVen, with her smelling all good and me rubbing that juicy ass, you know my dick is hard. Every time I'm around her, I stay ready to bust it open. But that ain't what she needs tonight. Before getting with RayVen, I ain't had to waste no time getting to know females too deep. Just fuck and keep it moving. In this last year and some change, she's been schooling me on how to love her. For a minute, I thought she was just being difficult, until I had a long talk with Mama Armateo. And she opened my eyes to some shit I hadn't realized.

I remember a few weeks after X was born I noticed something was wrong. Seems like every time X started crying, RayVen would start crying. I'd change his little shitty diaper and he'd go back to sleep. But she still would be balled up on the couch crying. Believe me, a nigga was lost so I called up Mama Armateo to help me with that too. I swear that woman is the plug when it comes to dealing with my wife. She rolled deep with Armateo for decades so I know she could help me with making this marriage thing work.

After explaining what was going on, she told me RayVen was going through some shit called postpartum depression. And put me on to some shit I could do to make her feel better. So while she was fighting that shit, I took over making sure X was straight. Ty helped out with keeping the house situated and he'd baby sit when I was taking care of RayVen. When I was alone with her, I'd run her a warm bath to get her to relax. Rub her down nice and slow with her favorite lotion. Made sure she was eating like she was supposed to. Eventually, she was able to snap out of it, and I was glad to have my girl back. But when everything calmed down with X, I noticed she was fighting something a little deeper than that.

She tries to hide it, but I been around her ass long enough to know when some shit is bothering her. I know deep down RayVen is scared of me flipping on her like that muthafucka she was married to before me. We had a deep conversation one night and she told me everything that muthafucka put her through. The one thing that will forever be stuck in my mind is the night my crew hit me with that 911 call saying that muthafucka showed up at her office. Every time I think about how she looked lying on the floor with her face all bruised up, covered with blood, barely breathing. Or in that hospital bed with her eye swollen shut and stitches in her lips. They had all types of IVs hooked to her arm so she could stop hurting. There ain't a day that goes by that I don't wish I could dig that nigga up and beat his ass all over again. I still say death was too good for his ass. At least we made him suffer.

Even though I hate to see her feeling down about herself, I don't give her any shit for it. I know it's my job as her man to never make her question where she stands with me. The last thing I want is another muthafucka stepping to her telling her how fine she is. That's why I make sure she hears it from me first on the daily. As sexy as my wife is, I know I can't stop other niggas from scoping out her fine ass. But I'll drop kick any muthafucka who tries to lay hands on her though. Better glance and keep it moving. I'm not playing that shit.

Eventually she starts snoring a little bit, and I lean down to kiss her forehead. Yeah, she a pain in the ass sometimes, but I meant every word of what I said earlier. I'll go hard to make sure she and X are safe.

With my crew still being shook about what went down yesterday, I decide to give everybody a few days off to get their minds right. The police hit me up earlier to let me know they were still investigating the building. From the minor work we'd gotten done, that place shouldn't have blown up the way it did. And with that dude Mariano or Marciano just popping up the way he did, something about that shit seemed kinda suspect. I ain't been out the game that long not to notice something wasn't right about that dude. Until I get a handle on things, I'm gonna definitely keep my eyes open.

I have my own office set up a few blocks away from the house for when I'm not at a job site. My father-in-law helped me get things set up and put me on to how to keep track of my employees and all that other bullshit. I asked him to keep track of my books at first because I didn't want the headache. But when I saw how easy I caught on to the shit he showed me, I took over doing it myself. It can be aggravating at times trying to figure out a budget for expenses, keep track of payroll, and all this bullshit with taxes. But it comes with the territory of running your own. And I ain't wanna run the risk of another muthafucka knowing more about my business than I do. I was chilling at my desk getting everything set up for payday when my phone goes off.

"Verano," I say into the receiver. After a few seconds of silence, I notice it's the same muthafucka from last time, breathing on the other end. "If you got something to say muthafucka get it off your chest, bruh."

"See that's your problem, homes. You always think you running shit. But you in over your head with this one fam."

"Is that right? Since you got my number you already know where I'm at so get at me…I ain't running."

"Oh, I will muthafucka…soon enough. You lucky them lil' muthafuckas you work with got out the building on time. That was a close call."

It finally dawns on me that this muthafucka had planted something in the building that day. "Nah, you the one that's lucky muthafucka. Stop hiding behind a phone and face me, or are you too much of a bitch to talk shit in person."

"On my terms homes…I got some other shit to handle before then."

"Yeah, whatever muthafucka." I start to hang up the receiver.

"By the way…tell RayVen I said wassup." Then his punk ass disconnects the call.

CHAPTER 7

RayVen

fter what I witnessed between Marianna and my supervisor a few days ago, it's safe to say that I've been avoiding both of them. Although, Marianna still seems to be itching for an ass whooping. Every time I walk by, she's cutting her eyes at me. Like damn, why are you trying so hard to be relevant. All you do is come to work, suck off the supervisor, and try to start shit. Find a fucking hobby. This is a business not Love and Hip Hop. Since I didn't have many sessions scheduled for today, I take X out of daycare and to a park not too far from the center. It never hurt for him to run around and get some fresh air in his lungs. There's a few other babies out here running around so they play with each other for a few minutes. While the other moms are on their cells or talking to each other, I'm watching my baby like a hawk. And I have no problem keeping eyes on the other babies in the area. Call me overprotective if you want to. But there are too many sick muthafuckas in this world who have no issue snatching the innocence from a child. All these hoes on the street willing to give it up for a dollar, but they take it from a baby. In my line of work, you wouldn't believe the number of children I've counseled who've been victims of molestation. Like with any form of rape it's not always a stranger. There's always some uncle, cousin, stepbrother, hell sometimes the child's own parent, who had been the cause of the abuse. I hate to say it, but it's mostly families of color who sweep that shit under the rug, pretending the abuse is not happening. Because they want to put up the pretense that something so vile could never happen in their family. I don't see how half of these women sleep at night knowing that the man they're having sex with is using that same dick to fuck a child. You would think they would notice the change in their child. The loss of innocence always has obvious signs. No, they just turn a blind eye because they just know *he wouldn't do that.* But if Grandma, Auntie, or Mama would have addressed the issue in the beginning, they could have prevented that child from suffering a lifetime of damage. There are so many days when I'm fighting back tears as my young clients describe how a person they were close to, hurt them on a daily basis. I shake my head, trying to ward off the negative thoughts.

X gets excited when he notices a swing set in the middle of the park and immediately runs over to them.

"Mommy, sing," he says, meaning he wants to get in the swing. "Please, Mommy sing."

I laugh as I lift him up, making sure he's safely in the harness. "Ok, ready?"

"Yeah! Push!"

I start pushing him, causing him to squeal with delight. The more I push, the more he screams. I never realized how much I'd enjoy being a mom until he was born. True, it was a rough nine months with all the morning sickness, mood swings, and cravings. Plus, Ty had just moved in with us and I was trying my best to make sure he was getting adjusted ok. I swear, if it wasn't for Xavien stepping up the way he did, I would have been an emotional wreck. It was rough having to get up every few hours to feed X and check his little dirty diapers. But seeing how much he's grown is so amazing. I still remember when he first started crawling, which didn't last long because he was walking soon after that. People are always surprised by how well he can talk at one year old. But I always read to him and began teaching him how to read by himself soon after. He already knows how to count, his alphabet, and a bunch of other things I didn't learn until kindergarten. Xavien has also been teaching him Spanish, which I wasn't aware of until he surprised me one morning.

I walked into his room to get him ready for school, and I didn't know he was awake already.

"Hola Mommy, como estas?" he said out of nowhere

"What did you say?" I asked him.

"Como estas?" he repeated.

"Muy bien, gracias y tu?"

"Todavía estoy dormido."

"Yo también, hijo."

When I tell you I was shocked that my baby is not only speaking Spanish, but he caught on quicker than I did. He's still having trouble with a few words, but he's young enough to get it right.

But for the moment, nothing in this world is more important than seeing that big smile on my son's face. When he's ready to get out, I take him to a miniature slide to let him have a few rounds with that. At the end of his third go around, he runs over to me holding the front of his pants.

"Gotta potty Mommy."

I take his hand, leading him to a nearby restroom. Once we both have emptied our bladders, it's time to grab something to eat. I got him some chicken nuggets, apple slices, and juice, while getting myself a sprite and chicken tenders. Instead of rushing back to the center, I sit down and enjoy my lunch date with my son.

"Mommy, where Daddy?"

"He's at work, sweet pea."

"Oh, I made him a picture."

I gasp. "You did!"

He nods proudly. "Uh huh…one for him and one for Ty."

I pretend to pout. "What about me? I want one too."

"Not finished." He stands up in his seat, grabs my face, and kisses me on the cheek. "Feel better?"

I continue to pretend like I'm sad. "A little bit."

"Muah!" He gives me another big kiss on the cheek, wrapping his little arms around me. I start laughing, causing X to touch my face. "Mommy…"

"Yes honey?"

"You pretty. I glad you my mommy." He hugs me again.

Why is my baby trying to make me cry in front of all these people? I squeeze him tightly. "Ready to go?"

"Yeah!"

"Yeah what?" I say putting my hands on my hips.

"Yeah ma'am!"

"Okay, that's better."

By the time we make it back to the center, X is knocked out, so I carry him back to daycare so he can get a decent nap in. When I finally get back to my office, I notice that my door is cracked, and there's another bouquet of lilies on my desk. I glance up the hall to the front desk and Marianna is nowhere to be found. Probably on her knees providing community service. Like before, there's an envelope with my name on it. My first mind tells me just to throw the shit in the trash, but I won't be able to rest not knowing what it says.

Had a dream last night where I was

tasting you. I can't wait to hear you

scream my name boo.

Signed,

Your Secret Admirer

I rip up the card and throw it in the trash. As I start to take the flowers down the hall, my phone starts ringing.

"It's a wonderful day at Epic Changes."

"Good afternoon, Sexy," he says.

I sigh heavily, recognizing it's the same person from last week.

"Listen, this shit is getting old. You've had your laugh, now I suggest you keep it moving."

He laughs a little. "Baby, I'm just getting started."

"If you don't stop harassing me, I'm going to call the police."

"For what, calling to check on you and sending you flowers? That's not nice, Sexy. I guess you ain't used to a man treating you right. Tell your husband to step up."

"Not that it's any of your business, but my husband treats me very well."

"Yeah, for now…but you know Chains could never stay faithful to one female. The only one he's ever had a soft spot for besides you… is Marianna. They used to hang tight back in Jersey."

"And how do you know?"

"'Cause, I was there boo. He had it bad for her but she turned him down. And now that's she's back in the picture, I know he wouldn't mind rekindling the flame."

"You're so full of shit."

He laughs again. "Okay sweetness, I'm just trying to put you on to what's going on in front of you. I just don't want to see a fine ass female get played."

"What the fuck ever, goodbye."

"RayVen…"

"What?!"

"You looked sexy as hell playing in the park with your son today." With that he hung up.

Oh, my fucking god! I can't believe this muthafucka was in the park with us. I don't give two fucks about him watching me, but now that he's laid eyes on my son…this shit has to stop. I pick up my cell and try to call Xavien but his phone goes to voicemail after a few rings. After sending him a text to call me as soon as he can, I reach in my desk to pull out my purse. Perfectly concealed inside a large pocket is my P938 9mm Glock. I check the mag to make sure it's fully loaded, plus I still have an extra mag just in case. If I didn't learn anything else from Xavien's brothers, I remember to always keep an extra clip with me. Because I'll really never know if and when I may need it. If this dude is crazy enough to follow me to the park with my son, there's no telling what else he has up his sleeve.

Then there was all that bullshit he said about Xavien and Marianna. My mind was so caught up with other things I forgot to ask if he really knew her. But before I go running with what some asshole has to say, the least I can do is give my husband the benefit of the doubt. He is probably just someone who is jealous of Xavien anyway. If that's the case, then he needs to find something better to do with his time.

When I go outside to put the flowers in the garbage, I see Xavien's car pull up in front of my building. Imagine my surprise when the passenger door opens and Marianna gets out of his car. I know damn well this muthafucka isn't riding this skank ass bitch around in his car. Where and when did he start doing this shit? If Xavien didn't have a good fucking explanation for this shit, I'm going back inside and getting my glock. Because this muthafucka had to be losing his goddamn mind.

The smug bitch walks by me, looking like the cat that swallowed the canary. "Thank you so much for everything, Chains…I mean Xavien," she says and saunters inside the building.

I'm not going to waste any time questioning this bitch because that's all she wants. The satisfaction of knowing she caused some issues between us. But that doesn't mean I can't kick my dumb ass husband in his ass.

"Baby, before you even trip, her car broke down and she was stranded on the side of the road, so I gave her a ride back. That's all it was."

"I don't give a fuck about that bitch or her car breaking down. My question is what the fuck all that has to do with you." My eyes were burning from the tears threatening to fall from them but I hold them back.

He tries to touch me but I shove his hand off. "Ray, I was coming to get X and she was stranded on the side of the road. She flagged me down to help her start her car. It wouldn't start so I just gave her a ride back. That's all it was, baby. You know me, I wouldn't play you like that."

"You expect me to believe that bullshit?"

"First of all, you gonna stop coming out your mouth at me sideways and second, believe me when I say ain't shit happen, you feel me."

I shake my head at him. At the moment, I don't know what to believe. "I need to be alone right now, I'll see you at home."

Xavien wraps his arms around me when I try to leave. "RayVen, as long as we have been rocking, have I ever given you any fuckin' reason not to trust me?"

I sigh heavily.

He turns me around to face him, "Have I?"

I only shake my head.

"As close as I am to you right now, do you smell perfume or any type of shit like that on me?"

"No," I say softly.

"Aight then, damn! You know me better than that. I'm looking you in the eyes right now and telling you I ain't do nothing foul with her. Trust me, aight."

I nod. "All right, but the next time you see her or any other female stranded on the side of the road, let that bitch walk," I tell him.

He starts laughing. "Yes ma'am. I ain't tryna get no hot grits thrown on my ass while I'm sleep."

"Better act like you know."

"Ole mean ass." Xavien leans in to kiss me, but I move my face in the opposite direction. He smirks at me. "Damn, it's like that? Better come here before I fuck you in the parking lot in front of everybody."

If he was crazy enough to go down on me while being locked up in prison, then I know his threat had some weight to it. I finally let him kiss me.

"You make me sick, you know that right."

"Yeah, you get on my damn nerves too."

"I need to talk to you about something later tonight though."

He nods. "Aight."

When we make it back inside, I'm relieved that Marianna is nowhere in sight. If she had said anything out of pocket towards me, I would have been on my way to jail. Although I still have my suspicions about Xavien's interaction with her, I decide to let it go for now. At the end of the day, I love my husband and I trust him. I can read him well enough to know when he's lying. But men have practiced the art of lying with a straight face. When he and X had made it safely out the door, I go to my office and try to end this crazy day on a positive note.

CHAPTER 8

Xavien

*N*ormally, I don't let dumb shit get under my skin. But when that muthafucka called me earlier playing games on my phone, there is no way I'm letting that shit slide. The muthafucka called my office talking shit, strike one. Then his dumb ass admitted to trying to take my boys out last week, strike two. But when that muthafucka had the nerve to let my wife's name come out his mouth, trust me it's a wrap for that nigga. Even though the police have been investigating what went down at the building, I ain't putting them onto this. What the fuck I look like calling the police talking about somebody leaving threatening messages. The fuck I look like? I fuck pussy, but I ain't never been one. The only fucked up thing about this whole scenario is I don't know who this nigga is yet, and he seems to have eyes on me. And if he's got eyes on me, then more than likely he's got eyes on RayVen too. I do a thorough check of my office to make sure nothing is wired or there aren't any cameras installed, other than the ones I had. So far, everything checks out alright. I then shoot Carmine a quick text to let him know we have a situation. If that muthafucka wanna get grimy, he can be sure I can show his ass how it's done.

When I get through with double checking everything, it's almost time for me to go get X from daycare. I am getting my shit organized before I lock up, when someone knocks on my door.

"Come in," I tell the person on the other end. I stay strapped so it doesn't matter who the fuck it is.

The door swings open and that Marciano dude comes waltzing in. I wonder what this muthafucka wants. "I apologize for coming by unannounced, Mr. Verano. I just wanted to see how you are."

"I'm cool. You coulda saved yourself a trip."

He laughs. "I just feel terribly about what happened to you and your men at my building last week." He reaches on the inside of his jacket and pulls out a check. "I hope that will cover the damages."

If he was expecting me to do flips over 100 G's, he must have had me confused with a broke ass nigga. I shake my head and give it back to him. "Like I said man, I'm cool. Dude that got hurt is recovering and that's all that matters."

"I see." He puts the check back in his pocket. "Would you be interested in doing some work for me in the future?"

I shrug, "Depends."

"I know you're new here Mr. Verano, but I have my hands in several establishments across the city. I provide them with the funds they need to increase their clientele, and they pay me a small fee every week for my generosity. Things have been going well for my associates and me over the years. But lately, like everything else in the economy, my prices have gone up. And some of these business owners think that I'm being unreasonable and have been refusing to pay the increase. And every so often, I have to remind them not to bite the hand that feeds them."

"What the fuck that got to do with me?" This dude ain't saying nothing. From the sound of it, he's just an overdressed loan shark. I've done business with dudes who ran global empires, so I ain't impressed with his low budget ass.

"Your reputation proceeds you, Mr. Chains Verano. Did you really think a man of your stature could come to my city unnoticed?" He laughs and shakes his head. "With the work you've done with Don Armateo in Jersey, I know you will have no problem giving me the upper hand I need to put the people of Atlanta on notice."

I smirk at him.

"I guarantee if you take me up on my offer, you won't have to worry about ever punching a time clock again. There's a guy on my payroll who I know will triple what you're making now by running your construction business for you. On top of what you'll be making while you handle certain clients for me. So, what do you say?"

I shake my head. "I'll pass, man. Me and mine ain't hurting for nothing."

"Oh, that's right, you have a family now. Your wife works at that center for those disturbed children, doesn't she? I've heard she's a gorgeous young woman. A little on the heavy side, but still pretty."

I take my gun out my back pocket and point it at this muthafucka's head. "Watch your fuckin' mouth when you talk about my wife muthafucka. You said what you had to say and I ain't interested. Get the fuck on."

He nods. I keep my gun pointed at him as he gets up and makes his way to the door. "I'll give you some time to think about my offer. Thank you for your time, Chains."

When I'm sure the muthafucka is gone, only then do I put my gun up. I knew since I first laid eyes on his ass that something was foul about him. But his voice didn't match the punk bitch who kept playing on my phone. I glance at my phone and I'd missed a call from RayVen. I'm heading that way anyway so I'll just wait until I get to her to see what she wanted.

I don't know why muthafuckas wanna try me with dumb shit this week.

A few blocks away from RayVen's job, I see a car with the hood kicked up on the side of the road. With all the bullshit going on in the world today, I ain't tryna stop and help nobody to end up with a gun pulled on me. So, I keep riding with the intentions of ignoring whoever it is. That is, until some female steps out in front of me waving her arms. Reluctantly, I pull over and see if I can help. The only reason I stopped is because I'd want someone to stop and help RayVen, if for any reason I couldn't get to her.

"Oh my gosh, thank you so much."

When I get a closer to her, I notice it's Marianna. *I should have kept driving.* "No problem."

"I don't know what happened. It started stalling, so I pulled over, and now the stupid thing won't crank."

"You got jumper cables?" I ask keeping as much distance between me and her as possible.

She runs to her trunk to go get them.

After we get them hooked up, I try to give her battery a jump. We sit there for damn near ten minutes, but her car shuts off right after it's been jumped. Hell, I tried. If I had time I probably would have gotten her car straight for her. But fuck it, she ain't my woman. And I ain't tryna get caught up in no bullshit. Wifey sweet, but she also gotta bad ass temper.

"I'm sorry about your car, but you might have to get somebody else to check it out."

She shakes her head. "Ok, do you mind giving me a ride back to work? You're heading that way, right?" Marianna asks. "I only came out this way for my break and this shit happens. Please Chains, I don't wanna lose my job."

RayVen gonna kick my ass, I thought as I motion for her to come on.

She smiles as she grabs her purse and hops in the passenger seat.

The whole way back to the center, I feel Marianna staring at me. I swore to myself as soon as she comes at me out of pocket, I'm putting her ass on the side of the road.

"So, how long have you been married?" she asks.

"A year and some change."

She nods. "I figured it hadn't been that long. Is that why you left Jersey?"

"Something like that."

"Well, I hope she treats you right. I remember back in the day hoes used to be sweating your ass left and right. You couldn't say the name Chains without making a bitch panties get wet."

I ignore her comment.

"Do you think we can hang out sometime for old time's sake? I'd love to hear what's been going on with you all this time."

"I don't fuck around on my wife."

"Hmm…that's funny," Marianna says. "It doesn't seem like RayVen values your marriage as much as you do."

"What the fuck you mean by that?"

"She didn't tell you?" Marianna shook her head. "It's none of my business but I'd definitely want my husband to know if some mystery man is sending me flowers unless…Well, it could be nothing."

At that moment, I'd just pulled up to the front of the building to see RayVen walking from the trashcan.

"Chains, you're too good of a dude to let some female play you. Watch yourself around her, alright."

Although the shit Marianna said didn't sit well with me, I'm not gonna give any weight to anything coming out of her mouth. It's more than obvious that she's jealous of wifey and just wants her spot. Besides, RayVen has never given me any reason to question her. If somebody was pushing up on her, I'm sure she would tell me. But that was the least of my problems. With the way RayVen was looking at my ass, I had to dead that shit with the quickness. As fucked up as the situation looked between me and Marianna, ain't shit happen between us and it never will. After a few minutes of explaining what went down, I thank God I was eventually able to calm her down.

Since I know I'm treading on thin ice with her, I decide to make sure X is situated by the time she gets home. Plus, I gotta hot bath waiting on her so she can relax. I'm confident that she won't flip on me for that shit earlier, but I ain't want no type of bullshit to creep up in her head. She was already feeling insecure about herself, and I ain't wanna add to that shit. I definitely don't want her to feel like she gotta compete with anyone. The way I see it, there's no female that can compete with her anyway; especially Marianna. I still can't remember how I know her ass.

From the way my baby is smiling when she sees the setup I had in the bathroom, I have no doubt that she already forgave me. I take her purse and sit it on the counter, as she takes in the rose petals leading from the bedroom to the bathroom. The smile on her face grows when she notices her favorite candles are lit and surrounding our jacuzzi tub.

"What's all this for?" she asks.

"Just 'cause," I tell her as I pull her shirt over her head and begin to undress her.

I kiss her neck while my hands travel behind her back to unfasten her bra. She sighs, enjoying the feel of her titties finally being free from their prison. Her eyes close when my hands slide inside the waistband of her pants. I rub that ass a few times before sliding them down her legs. I kneel down and kiss her thighs, allowing her to hold onto my shoulders as she steps out of them. Scooping her up by her hips, I carry her over to the tub and place her gently into the warm water.

"Why is it so hard for me to stay mad at you?" RayVen asks while running her fingers through my hair.

"Cuz you love me," I tell her.

She laughs. "I do, but listen, about earlier today…"

I lean in close to her and run my tongue over her lips, shutting her up. "Leave it in the past, baby."

She shakes her head. "But Xavien…"

I kiss her again until she sighs in defeat. "You stress too much just enjoy the moment."

RayVen sighs again, but says nothing.

After lathering up a washcloth with warm water and her favorite soap, I gently begin to bathe her. Since she carries the most tension in her back, I start there. The sweet smell of her soap floods my nose as I rub the washcloth down the back of her neck to the base of her spine. I rinse the soap out the cloth and fill it with water. RayVen moans softly as I squeeze the warm water all over her back. I don't stop until all the soap is gone from her chocolate skin. Before I get to the front of her body, I take a minute to massage her shoulders.

"You want me to stop?" I tease.

"Don't start what you can't finish." She flicks a little water on me, causing me to laugh.

After she's good and relaxed, I pick up the cloth and get back to work. I take my time working my way down the front of her body, paying special attention to those pretty ass titties of hers.

"Lift your leg up," I tell her after rinsing the top half of her body.

RayVen readily raises her foot to the edge of the tub.

I rub the washcloth down the length of her leg, being careful not to neglect the back of her thighs, calves, or ankles. She starts giggling when I wash her feet.

"Ticklish ass," I say, resting the cloth on the tub to begin washing her feet with my hands.

She bites her bottom lip when I begin applying light pressure to the middle of her foot. From the way she is moaning, I know I have her feeling right. After spending about ten minutes on the right foot, I start to show the left some love. When I'm done, I put a little more soap on the washcloth and work my way up to the center of her thighs. My fingers lightly stroke her clit, causing her to gasp when I'm washing off the soap. At first it was an accident, but after seeing her reaction, my hand gets a mind of its own. She grabs my arm when my fingers apply more pressure to that shit. I feel her thighs start to clench up around my hand, so I lean a little further into the tub allowing my two fingers to slip inside her.

"Damn X, why are you always doing this to me?" she moans.

I only smirk at her as I watch her body scoot further down into the tub, giving me deeper access to *MY* pussy. Some way or another, RayVen has freed my dick from my boxers. Next thing I know she's sucking the shit out that muthafucka. But a nigga stays focused. With my fingers still long stroking her, I curl them muthafuckas up and find that sensitive rim deep inside those walls. Even though she has a mouth full of dick, I can still hear her scream. Seems like the faster I tap that spot, the faster her mouth strokes my dick. The water is starting to cool off, but them walls are hot as a muthafucka. By the time that shit starts throbbing around my fingers, I was coating RayVen's tonsils with this nut. My other hand caresses her hair as I watch her sexy lips drain the last bit of juice out of me.

"How you feel?" I ask.

She giggles. "Definitely relaxed."

I nod. "That's what I was going for."

I help her out the tub and wrap her in a big towel to help her dry off. After giving her a few minutes to brush her teeth, I take her to bed and rub her down with lotion until she is knocked out. Before I get ready to clock out my damn self, I go through the house to make sure everything is good. The sound of a car outside causes me to peep out the window to see Ty backing out the driveway. *That lil' nigga must be running a marathon.* I shake my head and check the locks. On my way through the living room I hear something vibrating. *The fuck is that?*

I follow the sound and it leads me to RayVen's phone which is sitting on the coffee table. *Why the fuck is her phone going off at this time of night?* Before I trip, I figure it's one of the kids at the center trying to get in touch with her. So, I pick it up, ready to relay the message just in case it is an emergency, you feel me. But it wasn't a missed call or voicemail. Some muthafucka from an unlisted number had texted her.

Can't wait to see you again tomorrow, boo.

First of all, who in the fuck is this muthafucka? And why the fuck is he calling my wife boo?

Being the muthafucka I am, I text his ass back.

Nigga, who the fuck is you and why you hitting up my wife?

:)

I call the nigga, since he thinks I'm playing, but his bitch ass blocks the call. Instead of going back to bed, I sit in the living room with RayVen's phone in my hand reading over the message. The more I read it, the more pissed off I get. Next thing I know, I'm scrolling through her phone to see if there's any more shit in there. But after only seeing her work emails, calls from the job and texts from me and Ty, I put the phone back on the couch. For some reason, that shit Marianna said starts to creep in my mind. The last thing I'm dumb enough to do is trust her ass. But with this late-night text, what the fuck is a dude to think. I gotta get to the bottom of this shit ASAP.

CHAPTER 9

amn, I hate it when I sleep in.

I hop out of bed and jump in the shower with the quickness. Even though I'm nowhere near late for work, I've made a habit of getting up a little early to make sure breakfast is ready for my family, as well as getting a head start on getting X ready for daycare. But after the special treatment from my husband last night, I was out for the count. When I finally make it downstairs, Ms. Lana already has a buffet on the table. Waffles, biscuits, sausage, fruit, you name it, she's got it.

"See ya' later, Ma," Ty says to me. He's running out the front door, balancing a plate of food in one hand and his book bag in the other.

I only shake my head.

"Good morning, dear," Ms. Lana says. "Sit down and help yourself."

"Thank you. I'm sorry I overslept. I didn't mean to put you through any trouble."

"My dear, you do too much. Now sit."

I take a seat at the table and notice Xavien and X are sharing a plate. Ms. Lana places a plate of waffles, eggs, and sausage in front of me.

"You boys ok over there?" I ask them.

"Yeah, Mommy!" X says.

But all Xavien does is nod in my direction, which is unlike him.

"Hey, you ok?" I reach over the table to stroke his arm.

"Mm hmm," is the only thing he says.

He continues the silent treatment until X is finished eating, and then he carries him upstairs to get him dressed.

"Something is bothering my son," Ms. Lana says as soon as he is gone.

I nod. "I know. Did he say anything when he came into the kitchen this morning?"

She shakes her head. "Just good morning but no hug like he usually does." She sighs heavily.

"Thank you for fixing breakfast for us." I get up from the table. "I really appreciate it."

A concerned look crosses her face. "But you barely touched your food."

I nod. "I can't eat anything knowing he's upset."

I wrap my leftovers in foil and go upstairs to check on my husband. When I find him, he's still in X's room getting him dressed. The smell of soap floods my nose letting me know he just gave him a bath.

"Need a hand?" I ask.

"I got it," he says flatly.

I sigh. "Xavien, please tell me what's bothering you. After last night, I thought things were ok between us. Now it seems like you're upset with me."

He takes a deep breath as if he's trying to compose himself. "You know somebody texted your phone last night."

"Really...?" I ask genuinely surprised by what he said. There have been a few occasions where a few of my kids or someone else I was counseling contacted me late at night. That's why Xavien has the password to my phone. Just in case I'm asleep when they contact me during an emergency. Plus, he knows I don't have anything to hide. But don't get it twisted; the day I gave him mine, he gave me his.

"Did they say who it was?"

"Nah..." he says. "They was just calling you boo and shit."

"Well, I'm nobody's boo but yours...it must have been a wrong number or something."

Xavien stares at me for a minute and then nods. "Yeah..."

I give him a kiss on the cheek. "Trust me, you don't have anything to worry about...I'm all yours."

"Me too!" X says excitedly.

I laugh and give him a kiss on the forehead.

About a half an hour later, X and I are pulling up in front of the center. Imagine my surprise to see a very official looking SUV parked in front of the building. When I get closer, I notice it's a 2017 Ford

Expedition with black tint on the windows. Two men are standing outside of the vehicle making light conversation. Both are wearing suits, shades, and gloves, reminding me of the men in black. But my guess is they are security for the owner of the vehicle. *This should be interesting*, I think to myself as I take my baby to daycare. Thank God he doesn't start with one of his tantrums today. Instead he gives me a big hug and a kiss, which I'll gladly take any day.

While walking down the corridor, I see Tanya waving to get my attention. I have no idea what she wants, so I just wave back. She then motions for me to come to her office. The second I step inside, she looks around as if to make sure no one is watching before closing the door.

"Girl, do you have any idea who Tim is in his office talking to?" she asks.

I only shrug. "No clue."

"Marciano Barajas."

"Ooh kay…" I have no idea who that is.

"Girl, Marciano is one of the biggest philanthropists in Atlanta. He's donated millions of dollars to businesses all over the city. Word has it, he wants to contribute to the center."

"Wow, more exposure for the center would be a blessing. That way we can reach more communities and help more kids."

She nods. "But you know your friend is right there in the middle of the meeting, right."

"Who?"

She rolls her eyes and smacks her lips. "Marianna. I don't see what that skank bitch has to do with an investors meeting, but Tim insisted that she needed to be involved."

"Hmm…" is all I can say.

"Between you and me, I think he's fucking her."

"Wouldn't surprise me at all." Even though I trust Tanya, I'm not spilling any kind of tea about what I witnessed last week. The only thing that's going to do is add to the unnecessary drama around here. And having my name caught up in bullshit isn't my style. I chat with Tanya a few more minutes before continuing my journey to my office.

A few feet away from my door I see Mr. Mitchell and a well-dressed older gentleman chatting in the hallway. He appears to be in his late 40's, early 50's, probably Hispanic or something along those lines. Queen bitch is back at her desk on the phone, probably bragging about the amount of dick she just got through sucking.

"RayVen, perfect timing," Mr. Mitchell says as soon as he spots me. "There's someone I would like you to meet."

They both walk towards my office but I meet them halfway.

"Marciano Barajas, meet RayVen Verano. She's head supervisor of our juvenile division."

"Ay RayVen. Encantada de conocerte," he says.

"Mucho gusto. Igualmente," I reply.

He smiles even though I can tell he's a little taken back that I understood what he said. Yes, a bitch speaks fluent Spanish too, thanks to my hubby.

"Eres Cubano?" he asks. I guess my dark skin kind of threw him for a loop.

"No, no. Mi esposo es puertorriqueños."

Mr. Mitchell is looking back and forth between us. Clearly confused, because he couldn't understand what we were saying.

"Tim, would you mind if I talk privately with, Mrs. Verano?" Marciano asks still smiling at me.

"If it's ok with you, RayVen?"

I motion for him to step inside my office.

"How can I help you, Mr. Barajas?" I ask once he's seated at my desk and the door is closed.

"Please, call me Marciano," he tells me. "Before you talk with Tim about our meeting, I wanted to share my ideas with you first hand."

I only nod.

"I think you all do a fantastic job with how you handle these kids but with so many requiring help, I would think you would need a bigger facility. That way it's not so cramped with all the growing teens you have here. Plus, with the center being located so close to the heart of Atlanta, they can be easily influenced by so many negative elements."

Again, I nod.

"Now, my plan, should I invest, is to have a bigger building constructed specifically designed for the needs of the children. A more secluded location so they can work on whatever issues they're dealing with."

"I see. So, what will happen to this building?"

"I haven't decided yet, but I'm sure I can think of something that will be more substantial to the community."

"And Mr. Mitchell has agreed to this?"

"He's open to the idea of course, but I know with you on board we'll have no problem getting the ball rolling."

I may not have been as street smart as my husband but it's clear that this guy is a snake. A blind man can see he doesn't give a shit about these kids or improving this center. He just wants to use this building for his own selfish reasons.

"Mr. Barajas, the reason this building is located in this area is so it can specifically cater to the kids of this city and surrounding communities. This is where they feel the safest and it's at a reasonable distance. Not too many of these kids can afford to travel to some undisclosed location where they will more than likely feel as if they're outcasts. And the last thing I'm going to let anyone do is make them feel negatively about themselves."

He only nods.

"Now, if you had suggested that we expand and create another branch of the center along with keeping this one up and running, then I would have been interested. But in what way can you guarantee that these children will benefit from your investment?"

He smiles at me. "My word is my guarantee, RayVen."

"Well, I can't jeopardize the livelihood of these kids with empty promises." I walk over to the door and open it for him. "Have a good day, Mr. Barajas."

He gets up without a word, taking my cue that he needs to leave. "Thank you for your time, RayVen."

I shake his extended hand and watch him walk towards the exit. It's no surprise when I notice him stop at the front desk and whisper something to Marianna. She starts giggling in response. I close the door to my office and shake my head.

Scandalous bitch.

CHAPTER 10

Xavien

$\mathcal{I}$t's Monday morning, which means me and my crew are back to putting this work in. Everyone's nerves had finally calmed down, so we were focused solely on stacking this paper. Mike hit me up about wanting to return to work this week, but I told him to chill and focus on getting his health on track. He's a strong worker, but I don't wanna run the risk of him coming back too soon. There's always the possibility of aggravating the injury or him hearing a loud noise and flipping out. And that's some shit I can't have. This week we're handling a small remodeling job. A popular soul food restaurant wanted an upgrade so they hit us up to handle the job. I remember taking RayVen here one night after work because she didn't feel like cooking. I ain't gone lie, the food was blazing. That macaroni and cheese, fried chicken wings, and cornbread had us done in that night. Plus, with the amount of food they served, the prices were worth paying. So, I can see how they reached five-star status when they were up and running.

Speaking of my apple head wife, I've been feeling kinda bad about the way I acted towards her. Even though I was trippin' over that late-night text, I shouldn't have been so cold to her. After asking her about it, she said it was probably just a wrong number or something. And I was starting to believe maybe it was. Besides, her phone hadn't gone off like that all weekend. But when it did, it was strictly work related or something that wasn't worth the stress. Since the restaurant isn't too far from the center, I thought it would be a good idea to take her out to lunch. Since I was man enough to accuse her of doing some shady shit, the least I can do is apologize.

So, around twelve I give everyone an hour for lunch and go to pick up RayVen. We would've brought X along but he was knocked out. And the best thing to do is let lil' dude get his nap in. I'd already called an order in on the way to get her, 'cause I damn sure don't feel like waiting the whole damn break just to get some food.

"So, how's your day going?" I ask her. We were sitting in the park enjoying the warm weather.

"So far, so good. I think Mr. Mitchell is about to get involved with something over his head though."

"What makes you say that?" I pass her the tray of French fries we were sharing.

"Some big shot stopped by the office last Friday, claiming he wants to invest in the center."

"Ain't that a good thing though?"

"Not if he wants to move the kids to some building in the middle of nowhere and use the center for his own selfish reasons."

I nod. Impressed that baby girl is getting better at judging people. "So, you peeped that out about him already?"

"Yeah, that dude is a snake and I'll invest in the center myself before I let someone toss those kids on the street." She pauses to take a bite of her sandwich. "How are things going at the restaurant, did Mike come back to work yet?"

"Nah, I told him to rest up. But other than that, things are going good. We should hopefully have it finished within the next few weeks."

This time she nods. "Well, just take your time and be safe, honey bun."

I laugh at her and shake my head. She's always coming up with an off the wall nickname for me.

We chill for a few more minutes before I take her back to the job. This traffic is no joke, and with it being lunch time this shit is ridiculous. Instead of just dropping her off, I take a minute to walk her to her office. That chick Marianna starts smiling as soon as we walk by.

"RayVen, there's a package for you on your desk," she says loud enough for everyone to hear. Like she couldn't just call RayVen to the desk and let her know.

RayVen just ignores her and keeps on walking. I watch as she unlocks her door but instead of going to her desk, she pauses in the doorway like something has her shook. The expression on her face doesn't sit right with me so I follow her inside. But what the fuck do I see? A big ass bouquet of flowers sitting on her desk. The vase holding the flowers has a big ass pink bow around it. And from looking at it, I know the shit was expensive. Not only did this muthafucka send her flowers, but there's a card kicked up on her desk with her name on it. While she was frozen like she's doing a mannequin challenge or some shit, I close the door as I step inside the office with her. At this point, I don't give a fuck about no lunch break. I wasn't gonna show my ass 'cause this is her work, but best believe I'm gonna get some fuckin' answers.

"Oh god, not again," she says finally.

"The fuck you mean, not again?" I ask sitting on the edge of her desk.

She sighs heavily. "For the past week or so, someone has been sending these flowers to my office."

"So, this shit been going on for a week but I'm just now finding out about it? Who the fuck are they from?"

She shrugs. "I don't know."

I snatch the card off the desk and read it.

Just wanted to put a smile on your face, boo.

Can't wait to see you again, beautiful.

Signed,

Your Secret Admirer

I ball up the card and throw that shit. "So, I take it this the same muthafucka who texted your phone last week?"

"Xavien, I don't know who texted my phone and I damn sure don't know who's sending these flowers."

"Well, it's obviously the same nigga 'cause I doubt there's two muthafuckas calling you, boo."

"But this person doesn't have my cell."

I stare at her for a minute, not believing this shit. "So, what the fuck you saying, Ray? This muthafucka been calling your job?"

"Xavien, please calm down."

"Calm down?! The fuck you mean calm down?! Another muthafucka sending my wife flowers and blowing up your phone and shit, and you expect me to be ok with the shit."

I can see tears forming in her eyes due to frustration, but right now I'm too fucking pissed off to care.

RayVen sighs heavily. "Believe me when I tell you it's not what it seems. Xavien, I would never."

I get in her face and she flinches like she was expecting me to hit her or some shit. Now, that really pisses me off. I've done a lot of fucked up shit, but never have I ever put hands on a female. "If it was like that Ray, then why the fuck you ain't tell me about this shit when it first started happening? At the end of the day, you been hiding shit from me. On top of accusing me of doing shit that you know damn well I ain't doing. That's foul as fuck you don't even trust me, Ray."

She nods. "I wanted to tell you earlier but I didn't know how."

"By opening your fucking mouth, that's how." I shake my head. "I don't have shit else to say to your ass right now."

I pick up the big, beautiful vase of flowers and throw that shit into a wall. On my way out the building, I notice Marianna sitting at the desk smiling like she's the joker or some shit.

"So, I take it those flowers weren't from you?" she says. "Oops my bad."

If I was into beating women, I swear I would've punched the bitch dead in her mouth, but I just keep it moving.

When I make it back to the restaurant, I see everyone had started back working already, which is cool with me 'cause I ain't want to flip out on nobody 'cause of my personal shit. This shit just doesn't seem real. I can't believe RayVen had lied to me. If somebody was coming at her sideways, she knows all she gotta do is come to me and I'll dead the shit. What the fuck is she tryna do, protect the nigga or some shit?

When I finally have my mind right, I go back in the building and focus on getting it situated. I ended up working out all my frustrations on that muthafucka too. For a minute, everybody just stopped and stared at me. I was single-handedly throwing sofas and tables around like they weren't shit. But they were smart enough to stay the fuck outta my way.

Ty eventually comes over to see what was up. "Yo X, you good?" he asks.

"I'm straight, fam," I tell him.

He nods. "Aight, lemme know if I can do anything."

We bust our ass until about six that evening, before I finally tell them to go on home. As usual, I wait until everyone else leaves before locking up and heading to my car.

"X, you mind if I ride with you?" Ty asks.

"No action lined up tonight?"

"Nah, I gotta test coming up and I ain't tryna fail that shit."

I nod. You can say what you want about lil' dude, but Ty has his head on straight. He may run the streets a lot, but he busts his ass at work and he's passing all his classes. If I'd had that mindset when I was his age, I wouldn't have gone down the road I did.

"So, what you and mom dukes get in a fight about?"

"Who says we had a fight?"

"Dude, the way you was throwing shit around at the restaurant, something serious had to be on you. And can't nothing get you that mad but RayVen."

I shake my head. This lil' nigga was too smart. "Aight, if I put you onto something, you promise to keep it on the low?"

He nods.

"Somebody been sending flowers to her job and calling her. I think it's the same muthafucka who's been calling me talking shit."

"Hold up, you think she's fuckin' with this dude? Mom dukes don't roll like that, X."

"That's what I know. Something about this whole situation ain't sitting right with me. Like somebody tryna start shit between us on purpose."

"Damn, hating ass muthafuckas. Anybody come to mind?"

I shake my head. "Could be anybody. Until my fam comes through to scope shit out, keep your eyes open. Them muthafuckas got eyes on all of us."

He nods. "I got you fam."

RayVen would probably flip if she knew Ty has a gun, but I'm just covering all my bases. When my brothers came through to visit a while ago, we took him out with us so he can learn some shit. I know he loves the shit out of RayVen. So, I can trust him to do what he needs to do to keep her safe when I'm not around.

When we finally reach the house, I see her car is already in the driveway. I wasn't really in the mood to talk so I head straight for the shower. It's crazy you don't realize how sore your body is until you get underneath that hot ass water. So, I stay in there for a good minute just soaking and shit. After getting cleaned up, I go see about X. It's crazy; he can't sleep unless he lays eyes on me and his mama. If one of us is gone too long he will show out. I know RayVen had already read him a story so I just chill with him until he falls asleep. Once he's tucked in, I go to one of the spare rooms and chill in there. Even though I'm pretty sure RayVen didn't fuck anyone else, she still lied to me. And that shit kinda hurt, you feel me. I thought we were past this bullshit. If she doesn't trust me enough with something that deep, then what does that say about how she fucks with me?

I was playing a game on my phone when a text comes through from Carmine.

Sup Bro?

Chillin' fam, wassup?

Gotta crew that just touched down in your area. If there are eyes on y'all then they will definitely scope them out.

Tony and Enzo with them? I ask him

Tony and Enzo were the only dudes in Armateo's security that I roll with. They started working for him around the same time I did. Not only are the muthafuckas crazy as hell, but they on point with their shit. Whenever I needed to handle a heavy situation, they had my back. The last time I hit them up was probably about two years ago. They were the ones who put me onto that muthafucka at Ray's job. And the ones who helped put that muthafucka on a missing person's list. If I was gonna have anyone watching my back besides my bros, it would be those two.

Nah, they on a break, but they said if we need them to hit them up.

Damn, aight. Just make sure they have eyes on RayVen. Some shit has been going down at her job.

We got all y'all covered, fam. Trust me. What's been going on at her job?

Some muthafucka sending her flowers and shit. Been hitting up her office phone. Even texted her cell.

Damn, anybody shady at her job?

Just some chick named Marianna. She's been tryna push up on me. SMH. Says she's from Jersey.

LOL. Even when you locked down these hoes don't care. My girls are still in their feelings about you being married.

LMAO, they'll be aight. I ain't going down that road no more.

KMSL. Pussy whipped ass.

Fuck you, nigga. When y'all coming down?

I'll let you know when we touch down. We gotta move so these muthafuckas don't know what hit 'em. If they know you, then they definitely know me and V.J.

Feel you on that shit.

There's a light knock on the door and I look up to see RayVen walking in.

Hit you up later, fam.

Damn, you might as well sleep in the pussy.

LMAO, I reply before putting the phone on the nightstand.

"You're not coming to bed?" RayVen asks. From the worried look on her face I know she is probably wondering who I was texting.

"Nah. I'm cool where I'm at."

"Oh, ok." I'm tryna be hard but that hurt expression on her face is killing me. "Xavien, I have never cheated on you. I know I should have been honest with you from the beginning about what was going on, but I thought maybe it was just someone playing a joke or something."

I nod. "Better get some rest; we both got a long day tomorrow."

She drops her head in defeat. "Goodnight, Xavien."

I wait until she closes the door before switching off the light and trying to go to sleep.

CHAPTER 11

Without my husband lying in bed next to me, I ended up tossing and turning all night. I hate when we have a disagreement of any kind. And even more when we end up sleeping separately. While staring through the darkness at the walls, I couldn't help replaying the events of yesterday over and over in my head. I may have been clocked in five minutes before my coworkers started calling me for assistance. Apparently, two of the older kids had gotten into a really big argument and were close to coming to blows. Since Mr. Mitchell was cooped up in his office on a "business" call, they asked me to mediate the madness. After spending an hour with both kids, I was able to successfully defuse the situation. Then at around noon, Xavien texts me saying we're going to lunch. And after all the chaos I'd just dealt with, time away from the office is exactly what I needed.

On the way out, I noticed Mr. Mitchell was still in his office and of course Marianna was nowhere to be found. Anyway, Xavien and I had an awesome lunch date. It was nice just to share an outing discussing how our day is going so far. The highlight of the afternoon was seeing my husband's gorgeous smile. Especially, after how moody he's been all weekend. Although I still have no idea who texted me that night, it was still kind of cute to see him get jealous. But I'm not trying to take that too far. By the end of our date, I would have thought that little storm cloud had passed over us. Boy, was I wrong.

I should have known something was up when that hating ass bitch broadcasted there was a package in my office. But at the moment I was too focused on enjoying the last few minutes of my break with my husband. And, I don't pay attention to that bitch anyway. Honey, when I tell you my heart stopped when I saw those white lilies on my desk. If I could have disappeared for five minutes, I gladly would have. So, not only did I have to deal with the continuous bullshit of some unknown idiot, but I have to explain to a 6'3" pissed off Puerto Rican that I didn't know who the flowers were from. Lawd have mercy. In my defense, I honestly have no idea who sent them. But how do I convince my husband without sounding guilty?

From the way he flipped out and threw those flowers into the wall, I would have bet money that I was next in line. Don't get me wrong, Xavien has never put his hands on me in a violent way. But my experiences have taught me to never say never. On the other side of all that yelling and screaming, I know he was hurt. I'd broken my promise to never keep a secret from him. And no matter how fine a reason I had, it was wrong of me not to mention it sooner. I hate when Big Papi is mad at me. However, no matter how bad I want to fix this, the only thing I can do is leave him be. One thing I learned about my baby, is he's stubborn as hell. And if he doesn't want to talk, his ass isn't talking. You'd be better off trying to get a dog to lay eggs. But I did leave him a note just to tell him how much I love him. The last thing I want is for him to go to work and hurt himself, just because he isn't thinking straight. I'd never forgive myself.

Speaking of not thinking straight, I'm at work staring out the window instead of finding something useful to do. I glance at my reflection in a nearby mirror and shake my head. I look pitiful as hell right now. Eyes all sad with my lip hanging because I miss my husband. What makes things worse, is I don't have anything to keep me occupied except a bunch of paperwork. A few of my coworkers got together to take the kids on a field trip to an amusement park. All of us wanted to do something nice to show the kids how much we care about them, but of course money for the center is limited. So, Xavien and I pooled in the money they needed and made it seem like it was from an "anonymous" donation. That was back when he was speaking to me though. But, back to my little pathetic self, I'm still sitting here staring out the window when there's a knock on the office door. Absently, I tell whoever it is to come in. Then all of a sudden, I hear...

"Bitch, you know damn well you ain't doing no work!"

If I had spun around in my chair any faster, I would have been on the floor. "Oh my god, B!!" I jump out of the chair and rush to give him a hug.

The last time I saw Bryan had to be a few months after X was born. He got a promotion at his job which required him to travel more. Plus, he recently reconciled with his mother and they were trying to start over. Oddly enough, her health took a serious nosedive after that. She was unfortunately diagnosed with breast cancer. With her unable to work and tolerate chemotherapy at the same time, he became her primary caregiver.

"What are you doing here?" I ask finally.

"Girl, I tell you that oncologist we were seeing ain't worth a pile of fly shit. So, we were recommended to a facility on this end to see if their treatment will help. Mama's been in the hospital all week getting medicine."

"You've been here all this time and you're just now letting me know you're here? You ain't even right."

"Now you know if I was able to come see my Ray sooner, you know I would have been right here. But these meds have had Mama going through it."

I nod in understanding. "I'm so sorry, B."

"Anyway Bitch, who told you to move out here and grow some hips?" Bryan takes a step back so he can twirl me around. "I guess it's true what they say. Soon as a bitch start getting some good dick from the right man, she gets thick as fuck."

"Chile, shut up!" I close the door so we can talk in private.

"Am I lying though? From the way that ass looks, Xavien must be tearing them walls up!"

I pick up a pillow and toss it at him. "Bitch, your mouth still doesn't have a filter."

"You know it."

We spend a little while catching up the best we can in the short time that he is here. Before we know it, a whole hour and a half has gone by.

"By the way, who is that snotty ass bitch at the front desk?" he asks suddenly.

I roll my eyes. "Our new receptionist."

"Hmm…well the only thing that bitch is gonna be filing is disability when I break her damn neck."

I burst out laughing. "What happened?"

He tells me about how Marianna copped an attitude with him when he asked for me. "I started to tell that bitch to dial all 9's 'cause she was definitely fucking with the right one. What the fuck is her problem anyway?"

I take a deep breath and tell him about everything that's been going on these past few weeks. On top of everything I was worried about.

"Ray, I know you got hands so I don't know why you even pressed over that ho. Xavien ain't going nowhere. He loves you too much."

A smile makes its way to my face. "You think so?"

"Ray, don't make me slap you. He's not Jaylen's punk ass. True, y'all gonna disagree from time to time, but what y'all have is real. Don't let no spiteful ass bitch come between y'all."

I only nod.

"Besides, you know bitches got in they feelings when you took him off the market. So, they gone try to come at you because they jealous and don't want to see y'all happy. But you gotta remind yourself that YOU'RE. THAT. BITCH. And ain't no bitch flyer than my Ray…well except for me."

We share a laugh.

"Thanks, B. I really needed that."

He gets up to give me a hug. "Mama knows."

Since it's been so long, I take him by to see X. My baby is a little cautious at first, but he eventually opens up to him.

"Girl, he is too precious," Bryan says as I walk him back to the front entrance. "When you gonna try for that girl?"

"Chile please," I laugh. "I'm blessed with the one I have."

"Mm hmm. Are your tubes tied?" he asks.

"That is none of your business."

"Since when honey? I was there when you first hooked up with Xavien, when y'all got married, and when you got knocked up with X. So, I need to know when my niece is coming."

I shake my head. "No time soon. Why don't you get somebody pregnant if you want another baby around so bad?"

"If I can find the right bitch to lay this hammer to, I would. But I don't want no crazy baby mama."

"Amen."

I walk Bryan to his car and give him a big hug. Lord knows I hate to see my bestie go. Outside of my family, Bryan is the only one I can trust. And I know it's the same for him. Just to think our friendship began with me literally talking him off a ledge. I had no professional training then, I was just a young girl in college trying to prevent a fellow classmate from doing something he'd later regret. Even back then I had a knack for reaching people. I know it wasn't a comfortable situation, but God blessed me twice that night. First, by showing me what my true calling is, and second, by blessing me with a lifetime friendship. After promising we will do better to keep in touch, he is gone. Once I realize there isn't much else for me to do today, I decide to grab my baby and head on home.

As I'm closing my files on the computer, the phone begins to ring. I'd already switched it to voicemail so I just let the machine answer it. I hear it beep after a few rings.

"That's not nice, Sexy. Iggin' my call like that."

Are you fucking kidding me? I can't believe this asshole is leaving a message on my office phone. Instead of picking up the receiver, I just listen to what he has to say.

"It's cool, I know your man is lurking hard now that he's seen my flowers." He laughs a little. "That's why I ain't call that day. I wanna meet up with you one day soon, boo. I think we need to talk face-to-face. I know Chains ain't gon' wanna talk to me, so maybe you and me can squash this shit."

Despite my better judgment, I pick up the receiver. "Where would you like to meet?"

He chuckles again. "There's that sexy ass voice. There's a farmer's market not too far from you that I can meet you at. It's out in the open with lots of people. I figure we can talk there. Maybe around noon?"

I sigh. "Fine, see you then."

CHAPTER 12

Xavien

*I*t's Saturday morning, meaning the end of our second week working on this restaurant. Since it's the weekend we figured it would be best to get an early start so we can get the day over and done with. I think it's safe to say we should be wrapping shit up in another week or so. Especially, if we keep putting these early hours in. Which is one of the reasons why I fuck with the crew I hired. They have no problem putting that overtime in to get the job done. These dudes don't even trip about working on holidays or weekends. If I really need them to handle something, I know they got me. But there have been a few times when I had to tell them muthafuckas to get the hell on. I told 'em straight; y'all muthafuckas ain't gonna get burnt out on my watch. Better go drink or fuck something and keep it moving. They always laugh when I tell them that, but they listen because they know I'm just fucking with them. But in more ways than one, I get why they work so hard. It ain't been long enough for me to forget what it's like on the inside of a prison. I'll admit, my wife ain't the only one dealing with demons from the past.

I can't count the number of times I jumped out the bed at the sound of footsteps in the hall or a loud noise outside. When you're locked up, you learn to react fast. A minute too soon, and you can end up fucked in more ways than one, you feel me. On those nights, I'd get up to peep things out around the house. It's usually the garbage man or some other bullshit going on outside. Or Ty creeping through the house sneaking food out the refrigerator. Even though I know shit is cool around me, it takes a minute for me to go back to sleep. Most of the time, I end up working out for a few in the basement. After hitting the bag or pumping iron for an hour or so, I can usually take a shower and crash. But some shit is just hard to forget.

I'll never forget my first night in when those muthafuckas tried to punk me. Talking about I was too pretty to be in prison and they were gonna break me in. Mutha fuck. That. Shit. I ain't never been the one for that shit. Bitch ain't never been in my blood. I ripped the guts out of all four of them fools with no remorse. At least that's what they told me. I think I had some kind of post-traumatic stress, or whatever that shit is, from seeing mom dukes shot in front of me. So, when muthafuckas stepped to me sideways, I'd flip the fuck out. When I'd get my senses back, there was always a body or two laying at my feet. That first year alone, I might have killed ten muthafuckas before everyone got the idea not to fuck with me.

When I'd established that I was the most ruthless muthafucka in the prison, I could pretty much do what I wanted. But I was just low-key with the way I moved. I ain't never been a nigga to brag on my shit. I just let my actions speak for themselves. But the one benefit I did appreciate was the option to serve out the rest of my sentence in solitary. Most muthafuckas was hating because they thought I was on a power trip, once they found out I was down with Armateo. But that was their issue. Besides getting a piece of ass imported whenever I felt the need, I could go wherever I wanted at any time. I didn't like showering with those suspect muthafuckas. So, I always showered at night. My boy A.J. would come through and let me out so I could wash up real quick, then I'd go back in the hole. Speaking of which, he hit me up a minute ago about Johnson getting taken out when he tried to stop a prison break. All bullshit aside, Johnson was an alright dude. I hated to hear he went out like that.

The one thing I hated about being out that time of night is you could hear muthafuckas screaming. With everything being so chill at those hours, the shit would just echo throughout the halls. It was so loud sometimes it almost felt like you were walking through the gates of hell. The guards would be walking around like it wasn't nothing new. But the shit made me sick to my stomach. I found out later that half the guards were getting paid to let inmates snatch who they wanted. Where dudes fuck up is they don't dead that shit in the beginning. If you stay in your lane and keep a sharp blade on you just in case, then you good. But the ones who feel they gotta come in there bragging and popping shit about they from this set or another—you know the ones who front like they hard because they thought doing a bid was a cakewalk—yeah, those the same ones that end up in the infirmary a day or so later. I done seen plenty of muthafuckas laid out, crying with a nurse putting gauze on they ass 'cause the shit's been ripped out. Some muthafuckas had to learn the hard way that the game of survival was different behind prison walls. And I would've offed myself before I ever let that shit happen to me.

I eventually had to tell baby girl about it, and she helped me worked through it as always. So, if working crazy hours helps my crew to cope with they own demons then…fuck it. I can't be mad at that.

Around one, I tell them to pack up and get the hell on. They invite me to go drinking with them later tonight but I pass. I have too much shit on my mind to just kick back, you feel me. After everyone clears out, I take a minute to scope out the building and check our inventory. The last thing I wanna do is start the next week half ass. If we needed some shit, I could pick it up and have it set up already.

"You and your crew do excellent work," a voice says behind me.

I look in their direction and see Marciano walking in the restaurant. I really didn't have time for this fake muthafucka today.

"Something you need, bruh?" I ask him.

"Oh, I was just stopping by to see if you've given any thought to the proposition I made to you last week."

"To tell you the truth, that shit ain't even cross my mind."

He laughs a little. "Chains, how long do you think you can keep up this little front of yours? You're one of the most feared men in the game. Do you really wanna give up that much power just so you can repair restaurants?"

I step to this fool because he is definitely fucking with the wrong nigga. "If I was you, I'd be careful how you come at me muthafucka. Take your bullshit offer and go fuck yourself with it."

"I don't know if your wife mentioned it, but her boss Tim

Mitchell has been struggling to provide funding for their little center. Apparently, he's mismanaged their money a time or two, and now they're in debt. When he reached out to me about his dilemma, it really broke my heart."

It finally clicked that this is the muthafucka that RayVen told me about last week. "If you gotta issue with me muthafucka bring it this way, but don't fuck with my wife."

"Well, I tried to offer my services but she's just as stubborn as you are. She's really dedicated to helping those kids. It'd be a shame if something happened to the center."

This muthafucka is a bitch at its finest. Tryna hustle me into working for him by threatening wifey's job. I only shake my head at his ass.

"Dude, you ain't saying shit. And you gotta come a lot harder than that to get my attention."

He nods, takes a card out his pocket, and places it on the table. "If you should ever change your mind. Give me a call."

"Whatever, bruh."

I watch him leave before packing up my shit and locking the door.

During the drive home, my phone starts going off. I look at the ID to see Carmine's number on the screen.

"Sup fam?"

"We at the house, bro."

"Everything cool?"

"Nah, Ty found an envelope on your steps. I think you need to see what's in it."

"Aight, on my way."

I step on the gas and haul ass to the house. The first thing I noticed when I pull up in the driveway is that RayVen's car is missing. I know for a fact the center is closed today, and she stopped taking sessions on the weekends. So, where the fuck was she at? Before I trip, I figure maybe she went somewhere with X. When I get inside, I see V.J. and Carmine chilling in the living room. They stand as soon as they spot me. I give both of them a pound.

"Where RayVen at?" I ask.

"That's what we're tryna figure out. Ty's in the room watching a movie with X."

I go down the hall to his room. "Yo, you seen RayVen?"

"Earlier, she asked me to watch X cuz she had a meeting or something. Then a minute ago somebody knocked on the door so I went to see who it was. But there wasn't nobody there. Just a brown envelope."

"You see what was in it?"

"Nah, that shit was kinda suspect, so I hit Carmine up like y'all told me."

I nod. "How long she been gone."

"Been a minute. I tried hitting up her cell to check on her, but she ain't never hit me back."

All kinda shit is running through my mind right now but I manage to stay cool. "Aight, you cool with X?"

He nods. "Yeah, I got him."

I nod and go back into the living room with my brothers.

"I told V.J. to hit up security and see if they got eyes on her."

"Did y'all see what was in the envelope?"

He nods and hands it to me.

I don't think there's a word to describe how I felt when I opened the envelope to see pictures of RayVen with another dude. Whoever took these pictures made sure to keep the dude's face hidden. I could only see the back of his bald head. But there was no mistaking my wife. One picture showed her with her arms folded across her chest while she stared at him. The second, he had his hand on her arm. The last one, he was leaned in close to her like he was whispering some shit in her ear. Or about to kiss her.

I flip a nearby table over, breaking whatever the hell was sitting on top of it.

"I don't believe this shit!"

"X chill," Carmine tells me. "For all we know this a bunch of bullshit. You said somebody was coming at you. Maybe this is some kinda setup."

"Man, I ain't even tryna hear that shit. Who is that muthafucka?!"

"Security just hit me back. RayVen is on her way home," V.J. tells us. "X, just chill until we find out what went down."

I'm pacing back and forth in the living room like a caged animal waiting to strike. I can't see shit but red I'm so fuckin' heated. All I can think about is the bullshit she told me these past few weeks. She didn't know who the flowers were from. She didn't know who was texting her in the middle of the night. But had the fuckin' nerve to meet up with some random muthafucka as soon as my back is turned. Miss me with the bullshit, man!

The sound of her car pulling up in the driveway grabs my attention.

"X, lemme talk to her for a minute aight," Carmine tells me.

The alarm chirps on the side door when she comes in and he goes to meet her.

"Hey Carmine!" she says sounding all happy to see him and shit. Like she ain't been out doing grimy shit behind my back.

"Ray, we gotta issue," I hear him tell her.

"Is everything ok?"

"Not really."

I couldn't take too much more of this back and forth shit. I damn near run around the corner to where they were.

"WHERE THE FUCK HAVE YOU BEEN?!" I ask her.

RayVen takes a few steps backwards. I know she is caught off guard by the way I came at her. And there is no denying the fear in her eyes. Her lips start quivering as she looks from Carmine back to me.

CHAPTER 13

RayVen

I glance at my phone which reads 11:30, meaning I made it a little earlier than expected. Closing my eyes, I take a deep breath to gather my nerves before exiting my car. I may have walked a few feet before the smell of baked goods bombard my nose. As far as I can remember, this is my first time visiting a farmer's market. And I never imagined it would be so crowded. Vendors were lined up as far as the eye can see, with tents shielding them and their assorted goodies from the blazing sun. If the situation had been different, I would have gladly taken my time going through each station to see what I could take home. But food is the furthest thing from my mind. In a matter of minutes, I will be face-to-face with the person who's caused nothing but drama in my life for the past few weeks. I know it's crazy for me to confront this person alone. Believe me, my heart is racing a mile a minute. When Xavien finds out, I know he's going to kick my ass. Yes, I'm going to be open and honest about this confrontation today, and hopefully, I'll have some good news. It may not be today or tomorrow, but I'll definitely tell him when the time is right. He knows my schedule like the back of his hand, so I'm a little relieved that he went to work early today. I didn't want to make up a lie because he would have saw right through that. Not that I really blame him for being worried. I mean, I honestly don't know this dude from a can of paint. And what's to stop him from flipping out on me if he chooses. I may not have anyone physically with me, but my gun is locked and loaded just in case something jumps off.

I take a minute to glance down at my phone, which now reads 11:45. Since this fool still hasn't showed up, I decide to walk to the far end of the market where bread is being sold. The sweet smell of cinnamon raisin bread greats my nose, causing my mouth to water. My stomach growls a little and I realize I left the house without grabbing breakfast. I was so nervous that it hadn't even crossed my mind until now.

"Good morning, can I help you?" the vendor asks with a smile.

"I'm just looking right now," I tell her.

"Take your time; if you need anything, just let me know."

I nod as I watch her go to help another patron.

"Damn, I could spot that ass a mile away," a familiar voice says from behind me.

I turn around and come face-to-face with a bald, Hispanic dude. He was so close that I had to take a step back to see beyond his brown eyes. I imagine he's about 5' 10", clean shaven. He seems to be not much older than me. Under different circumstances, I guess I would have deemed him attractive. Trust me, he's nowhere near as sexy as my husband, but he's definitely cute. The sleeves of his t-shirt covered the canvas of tattoos that adorned both his arms. I turn my attention back to his face to notice his brown eyes brazenly roaming up and down my body. For some reason, those tattoos seem so familiar to me.

"Why you looking all nervous? You scared of me?" he asks, still smirking.

I cross my arms over my chest in defiance. There is no way I am going to let this dude intimidate me. I don't give a shit who he is. "I'm here aren't I?"

That smile spreads across his face and he steps towards me. I imagine it looks like an awkward dance between us, with me trying to keep some space between us, while he circles me like a vulture hunting prey.

"Mmm…mmm…mmm…Yes, you most definitely are here, boo. With yo' sexy ass. If Chains hadn't of snatched you up when he did, I would have gladly taken you off the market."

I roll my eyes. "Speaking of which, I don't have time to dance around with you. Can you get to the point of why you wanted to meet with me?"

He motions for me to follow him over to the park bench. I glance around to make sure there are still plenty of people around just in case I need a witness.

"I just wanna talk, Sexy."

Begrudgingly, I follow him to the bench.

"Ladies first," he says inviting me to have a seat.

"No thank you."

I don't know if I should be annoyed or concerned that he's still smiling.

"Long story short, your dude Chains fucked up a solid operation of mine some time ago. One of my homies lost his life because he stuck his nose where it didn't belong. It was my intention to handle that shit, but he moved before we could settle up with it."

"So, I take it you're from Jersey also?"

He nods. "Real talk, that's why I thought you should know about him and Marianna. Just in case something popped off behind your back."

"Xavien already told me everything about his past. Trust me, it isn't that serious. What else is there for me to know?"

"True, Chains did have a lot of females riding his dick. But Marianna was the one who got away. Back in the day, those two were known as the Bonnie and Clyde of our block. Even though some shit went down before they made it official. But everyone knew that she was gonna be the one to take him off the market."

I really didn't want to hear this bullshit. From what Xavien told me, being with me is the first real relationship he ever had. And I trust he wouldn't lie to me about that.

"And how do you know all this again? Did you and Xavien used to be friends or something?"

"Nah, when Chains started working for Armateo, he got too gassed up to notice niggas who hustled on the block like he used to. The muthafucka forgot where he came from and shitted on everybody who he figured was beneath him. Me and Marianna always been cool, so of course she confided in me when Chains dogged her out."

I shake my head. "That's very unfortunate, but from what I'm hearing, that was a long time ago. I think it would be best if both of you moved on with your lives. Xavien is not that person anymore, so just get over it."

He runs his hand down my arm when I try to leave. "Shit don't work like that in the streets, RayVen. It doesn't matter how long ago you crossed somebody; if you don't handle shit straight up, then people end up getting hurt. It's just like a turf war. If a dude was ever affiliated with a certain set and he leaves, he can never go back there or he'd be killed on sight."

"I still don't understand what this has to do with me."

He leans in close until I can feel his breath on my cheek. I take a few steps backwards.

"I just wanted to warn you. Jersey is no doubt Chains' turf. But since he moved here, he's stumbled into my back yard. Some heavy ass shit is about to drop down on that muthafucka. And I'd hate to see yo' sexy ass get caught up in the mix."

I'm smart enough to recognize a threat when I hear one. But I'm not afraid of him. I step close enough to get in his face. "The last thing you want to do is get on my husband's bad side. I suggest you do yourself a favor and leave my family alone."

He closes the space between us, and I feel his hand grab my ass suddenly. I shove him backwards as hard as I can.

"My bad, I couldn't resist that shit," he says with a laugh. My stomach turns when he licks the center of the hand that he grabbed me with. "Damn, I'd love to get in them guts right now. Got my dick hard as fuck."

"You're sick, you know that."

He nods. "That may be. When you get home, tell him my clapback game is gonna be strong."

"You gotta name to go with that message."

"Nolo, trust me he knows who I am."

I roll my eyes and leave him standing there without a word. I've wasted enough time entertaining his crazy ass. The crowd had thinned out tremendously, making it easy for me to make it back to my car. Once I'm on the inside, I notice I have a missed call from Ty. Poor thing is probably worried about me. I told him I was only going to be gone for a little while. When I finally make it into traffic, I already know it's going to take a minute before I make it home. While creeping by at a snail's pace, I rack my brain trying to figure out how I know him. Tattoos, bald head...Nolo. Then all of a sudden it seems like a light bulb went off in my head.

I remember back at the prison when I was still counseling Xavien. One night, I'd shown up late for our session because I had a previous meeting that ran over. Of course, he was pissed off and cussed me the hell out. After talking to the Warden, we both agreed it would be a good idea for me to go on home. So, I'm walking down the hall just minding my own little business and these alarms start going off. I later learned that meant someone was escaping. Which became obvious when three Hispanic prisoners came running down the hall towards me. Instead of going wherever the hell they planned on going, they saw me and started chasing me. Lord only knows what they had in mind to do to me. If it wasn't for Xavien they would have succeeded. Then when Xavien was carrying me to safety, Warden asked him what had happened, and I remember him saying, "She was jumped by Nolo and his crew."

"Holy fucking shit!" I say to myself at the realization. This dude is someone Xavien was locked up with.

I doubt very much that there are two dudes named Nolo with a chip on their shoulder. But there is only one way to find out. After forty-five agonizing minutes of fighting through traffic, I finally pull up to my driveway, which looks like a mini car lot right about now. There's Ty's Camaro, Xavien's Challenger and Dodge Ram, which doubles as his work truck, and V.J.'s Hummer. I squeeze my black BMW 7 series in the yard before grabbing my purse and heading inside. Surprisingly, Carmine meets me at the door before anyone else.

"Hey Carmine!" I greet him with a quick hug.

When I step back, I notice the worried expression on his face. "Ray, we gotta situation."

My heart drops. The first thing that comes to mind is the conversation I had with that nutcase earlier, and that something may have happened to Xavien. "Is everything ok?"

"Not exactly."

Next thing I hear is Xavien's heavy footsteps as he flies around the corner like a bat out of hell.

"WHERE THE FUCK HAVE YOU BEEN?!" he yells at me.

I'm stunned silent for a few minutes, because I have never seen Xavien so pissed off; especially at me. The more I looked at him, the more scared I became. His green eyes were almost black and his face was red. He has his fists clenched so tight, that the veins looked like they were going to burst out of his skin.

I take a minute to swallow back the lump in my throat, along with any type of lie that was coming to mind. Because it is clear he knows something. "I-I went to the farmer's market for a few minutes."

"FOR WHAT, TO MEET UP WITH SOME OTHER MUTHAFUCKA?!"

I shake my head, "No, it wasn't like that at all."

He starts laughing a little bit making me even more nervous. I watch him stomp over to the counter and snatch up what looks like a stack of papers. He then shoves them in my hand.

"Explain this shit, then."

My hands start trembling as I stared at the pictures of me in the market earlier. From the way these pictures were taken, they looked like he and I were on a date or something. That explains why he was so close to me all the time; that bastard had this planned all along. No wonder Xavien has lost his damn mind.

"All that bullshit about not knowing who was blowing up your phone and shit, but soon as my back is turned, you go sneaking around to meet up with this muthafucka."

Lord, please help me calm this man down. I pray silently. I try touching his arm. "Xavien, please listen…"

"DON'T FUCKIN' TOUCH ME!" He shoves me away from him so hard that I fall backwards into the wall.

Carmine steps in between us, he's probably as worried as I am that a fist would soon follow. I don't know when the tears started falling but before I know it my face is soaked. Being shoved into a wall didn't hurt as much as Xavien being the one who pushed me. After all this time, my worst fear is coming true. He starts pacing but Carmine continues to block him.

"Why the fuck you do me like this, Ray?" Xavien asks finally.

"Xavien, I swear...I have never..."

"Shut the fuck up, Ray!"

"Please...listen..."

"I SAID SHUT THE FUCK UP!" He punches a nearby wall, causing me to curl up in a far corner.

"X, go outside and chill before you do something you gonna regret man," V.J. tells him.

I hear the sound of keys jingling, then a door slams a few minutes later.

Carmine squats down on the floor next to me and begins rubbing my shoulder.

"Carmine, I promise I never cheated on Xavien...I would never do anything to hurt him."

"I know Ray. Can you tell me what this dude looks like? Did he slip up and tell you what his name was?"

I take a deep breath and tell him everything I can remember

about Nolo plus the phone calls I've been getting.

He helps me to my feet. "Alright, just try and calm down. We gonna get to the bottom of this shit, aight."

I only nod and he hugs me just like an older brother would. The only thing I can do is embrace him tightly as he allows me to shed tears on his shoulder.

CHAPTER 14

Xavien

I don't know how long I've been driving since I left my house. All I know is I wanted to get as far away from that muthafucka as possible. There is a lot of shit going through my head that I don't even wanna think about. Along with a pain in my chest that I wasn't used to feeling. I'd recently opened myself up to this love shit. And I hadn't realized how much that muthafucka can hurt until now. Somewhere along the way, I'd stopped to get a bottle of Henny. Now, I'm sitting in an abandoned parking lot. I'm knocking this muthafucka back straight as I chill on the hood of my car. This is the first time I'd hit some alcohol on this level in a good minute. Come to think of it, it was a little over a year ago. And the reason I'd started drinking heavy that night is over some bullshit with RayVen. Ain't that a bitch. I remember that shit like it was yesterday. I was chilling at her crib. Just got through beating that back in, you feel me. She was asleep but I wanted something to drink before I KO'd. Then I find out she was leaving Jersey to take a job here. But like always, she ain't say shit to me until I called her out on it. Crazy enough, that was the first time she said she loved me. And that shit hit me full force in the chest because I knew that she meant that shit. Man, I was fucked all the way up. Back then, I wasn't tryna catch no feelings. I knew what was going on between us wasn't the same thing I was used to. Any other time I would've walked away, but it was something about her rock head ass that made me say fuck it. I'ma try this shit one time. I put the bottle to my lips and take another strong swig out that muthafucka.

Shaking my head, I keep seeing those pictures of that muthafucka all over my baby. I mean damn, why she let the muthafucka get all on her like that? She should've known better not to take her ass anywhere by herself. True, I been taught her how to defend herself, but at the end of the day, she's a female. That shit could've went down an entirely different way. All I kept thinking about is what if that muthafucka would've brought some extra bodies with him. I doubt security would have got to her in time since they lost track of her in the crowd. Trust me, I lit into they ass about that shit. They could've easily snatched her ass. Then what? we would've been sitting here plucking while them muthafuckas could've had her tied up somewhere. Probably laying hands on her bruising up her pretty ass face. I ain't even wanna think about some sick muthafucka tryna force his dick in her. Ain't no dick going in my wife but mine. I don't give a fuck if I get bodied. I want her to keep living, but that pussy coming with me, fuck that.

I take another shot to the dome as my mind wanders back to when she tried explaining to me what happened. She tried touching me and I pushed her. Yeah, I wanted her hand off me, but I ain't mean to push her like that. The look on her face was enough to let me know that I fucked up with that one. Never have I ever put my hands on my wife like that. I guess in her eyes I'm no better than that other muthafucka. My cell starts vibrating and I pull it out to see a text from Carmine. Everybody had been blowing me up since I hauled ass earlier. But I just ain't feel like being bothered.

Bro, where you at?

Getting a drink, I tell him

You need us to come get you.

Nah.

Aight, X. Watch yourself.

I put the phone back in my pocket and knock back the rest of the bottle. The best thing probably would have been for me to take it on to the house, but I needed a minute to myself. There is a bar not too far from where I'm at, so I pull up over there for a few. Lately, shit just ain't been making sense to me. Seems like the more I try to do the right thing, the more fucked up shit starts happening. I mean, I ain't never stepped out on my wife. No matter how many females try to come at me. Not once have I thought about fucking around on RayVen. I'm always there for my son. I bust my ass everyday just to make sure we all get what we need. Shit, at the end of the day, I'm doing everything I'm supposed to be doing. WHAT THE FUCK? I swear, I ain't had this many headaches when I was bodying muthafuckas for a living.

Once I'm inside the bar, I notice it ain't too crowded, which is a good thing. I easily grab a seat at one of the booths in the back. There's a flat screen TV on that side that has a game on it. After ordering a beer, I kick back and watch for a minute. I had just switched into chill mode when I hear someone ask:

127

"Damn, why you look so stressed?"

I look in the direction of the voice to see Marianna standing a few feet away. *Damn, can my night get any fuckin' worse?* I take another swallow of beer and ignore her ass.

"Lemme guess…" she says, sliding in the seat across from me. "You and wifey had a fight."

"Something like that."

"You wanna talk about it?"

"Not with you."

"Come on Chains, me and you always used to stay up late talking about all kinda shit that was on our minds. You used to always get that same look on your face when you used to stress about how to help your mama pay her rent."

"How in the fuck do you know that?" I ask finally turning around to face her.

"I told you we used to rock heavy in Jersey. We were kids back then though," she says with a laugh. "My father owned that corner store a few blocks away from your mama's house, remember."

Crazy as it sounds, I remember that shit. As my memory kicks in, I see myself back on the block of my old neighborhood. At the time I was like 21-22. I'd been working for Armateo for a good minute by then. So, there wasn't too many people who didn't know me. Especially, when it came to females. I was juggling three, maybe four, females back then. Yo' boy was kinda reckless back at that age, but I was still smart enough to never smash raw. Out of all the females I was fuckin with,

I did fuck with Marianna a little more than the others. I wasn't in love or none of that shit. But the thought crossed my mind to see how far things could go. That is, until Carmine put me on to her coming by his club to fuck with him. From the way me and Marianna used to vibe, I ain't think she would try to play me for my brother, but he dared me to come by one night to see for myself.

What was crazy, was that was the same night she'd just kicked it with me. I peeped that she was on her phone a little more than usual. She claimed that it was her dad checking to see when she would be home. True, her dad was kinda protective of her. He was an older cat so I knew he was kinda old fashioned. But shit still didn't sit right with me. So, I dropped her off at her crib, but instead of going home, I waited a block or so away. I had my car in a spot where it couldn't be spotted so I wasn't trippin' about her seeing me. About fifteen minutes later, I saw her leaving out the front door with a different outfit on. She hopped in her dad's ride and took off down the road. I followed her all the way to Carmine's spot, just like he told me from the jump. Now at that point, I coulda went on home, but I wanted to see how far she would go with him. The bouncers knew me of course, so they didn't ask no questions when I came to the door. When I was inside I asked security had they seen her, and they pointed me to Carmine's office. So, I went up there and caught her sucking his dick. I already knew the door was gonna be open 'cause my bro was giving me a play by play of what was going down. She was so busy waxing him off that she didn't see me peek my head in and nod at him. Which meant good looking out. He nodded back, telling me, no problem. Any idea of me getting into a relationship ended that same night. I curved her ass when she tried hitting me up the next day. She tried hitting up Carmine after she couldn't get through to me, but he was done with her after she swallowed his nut.

I start nodding as I digest everything that went down.

Marianna starts smiling again. "So, you remember me now?" she asks.

"Yeah, I also remember you sucking my brother off that same night you was with me."

She gets this shocked look on her face. Nasty ass.

"What, you thought he wasn't gonna tell me?"

"Chains, I admit, I made a big mistake back then. I knew you was fucking with other females and I got jealous. But I respected the fact that you always kept it one hunnid with me. I should've done the same."

I nod. "It's cool, I ain't trippin'. Shit happens for a reason, you feel me."

She nods and leans onto the table so her titties were showing. "Do you think us seeing each other again after all this time is for a reason also?"

"Nah, that's probably a coincidence."

Marianna laughs even though I wasn't joking. "You still have that crazy ass sense of humor."

I shake my head and get up to leave.

"Wait Chains, don't go yet." She gets up, walking close enough to put her titties on me. I take a step back but she wraps her arms around my neck, resting her face in my chest. "Don't you miss what we had? I know I miss the feel of that big dick in my stomach."

For some reason, my vision starts to get blurry. I think the effects of mixing Henny and the beer I was drinking, is starting to catch up with me. Especially, since I ain't drink shit in a while. I fall back in the booth for a minute just to get my head right. Next thing I know Marianna is all over my ass. Kissing all on my neck and shit. She starts digging her nails in my neck.

"Marianna get the fuck off me." I push her back as gently as I could. I ain't wanna hurt nobody else tonight.

Instead of taking the damn hint, her crazy ass gets more aggressive. "Please Chains, lemme feel that dick one more time. I promise I can fuck you better than RayVen can."

The mention of my wife's name sobered my ass up real quick.

"I said get the fuck off me!" I damn near throw her ass on the floor. From the stinging sensation on the back of my neck I know her ass scratched me. "Stay the fuck away from me, aight!"

"Nigga, fuck you and that fat ass bitch!" Marianna says. "You don't deserve a real bitch like me anyway."

"You right, I don't deserve no section 8, sucking dick in a bathroom, no walls having ass bitch. Get the fuck on."

When I make it outside, the night air helps to sober me up a little more. But there is no way I am gonna make it home as fucked up as I am. Good thing my office isn't that far from here. I thank God I made it to my spot without the police stopping me. The last thing I need tonight is a fucking DUI. I learned quick that they don't play down south with that shit. Besides, it took too much to get my record clean to begin with. And I ain't tryna fuck that up. My vision starts to fuck up again after I park the car. But I manage to lock up once I'm inside and stumble to the couch before the room starts spinning. Fuck! I know I'm gonna be feeling this shit in the morning.

CHAPTER 15

RayVen

It's one in the morning and Xavien still hasn't come home yet. The only thing that gave me a little relief is that Carmine and V.J. haven't come back either. So, hopefully they are all together. I'm not sure there's a word to describe what I've been feeling since that big disagreement we had earlier. Never would I have thought things would escalate to that level. All I wanted to do this morning was bring an end to the drama that our family has been going through. But it seems like whoever is behind all this is hell bent on driving a permanent wedge between us. A part of me hopes I'll be able to forgive Xavien for pushing me earlier. It's not like it was his closed fist. But who's to say it won't escalate to that point sometime in the future. All of this is putting me in a bad headspace. At least I can say he hasn't cheated on me. Well…I just hope and pray that he hasn't. I tried calling him earlier but his phone went straight to voicemail. And I keep telling myself that he just needs time to cool off. The crazy part is, I'm used to the arguing when it comes to relationships. Hell, that's all I did with Jaylen the first few years of our marriage. Then I eventually stopped caring. However, with Xavien…I hate when we argue.

Seems like all the warmth has left my body since he's been sleeping in the other room all week. I miss the feel of his strong arms squeezing my waist as he holds me close to him. The sound of his voice when he whispers to me in the middle of the night. Having him deep inside me as he makes me climax over and over again. God! This shit isn't right.

Somehow, I managed to put X to bed earlier. I think it helped that Ty kept him occupied with movies and playing with him while everything was going on. The last thing I wanted is for my son to see his parents arguing. I thank God he's been sleeping soundly so far. He usually can't sleep if he goes too long without seeing me or his dad. The sound of the alarm chirping as the side door opens grabs my attention. I wait on pins and needles, hoping it's my husband; however, I see Ty walking around the corner a few minutes later. I guess the disappointment on my face is obvious because he comes to join me on the couch.

"You ok, Ma," he asks.

I fake a smile. "I'm fine."

Ty takes a moment to study me. "Did X make it in yet?"

I shake my head. "No, not yet."

He nods. "I was thinkin' since we got so much going on, I'ma chill with going out so much. At least until we find out who's behind all this bullshit."

Usually I would fuss at him for cursing in front of me, but I give him a pass tonight. "You have your own life to live Ty. You don't have to stop living it for us."

He shrugs. "It ain't no thing. I had fun kicking it with lil' X today, and I know y'all need somebody to keep an eye on him. That's what families do right? pitch in when shit gets rough."

This time I did give a side-eye but I end up smiling. "Yep, that's all part of being a family. We all have to look out for each other."

"Besides, it's the least I can do. Y'all the only family I know." Ty hugs me then. "If you need me just lemme know."

I nod and watch him disappear down the hall.

After spending a few more minutes watching the clock, I make up my mind to go to bed. When I reach the top of the stairs, I hear the distant sound of X crying in his room. I walk down the hall to find him sitting up in his crib. He stands up as soon as he sees me.

"What's the matter, sweet pea?"

He raises his arms and I pick him up. "I miss Daddy."

My fingers wipe away his tears while I fight back my own. "I know, I miss him too sweet pea."

"When he coming back?"

I sigh. "In the morning."

X stops sniffling and brushes the stray tears from his face. "Promise?"

"I promise, love."

He buries his damp face in my neck and I just continue to hold him. While walking back and forth through his room, I sing to him and stroke his back softly. Reminding me of when he became restless as a newborn. Eventually, he falls back to sleep. After tucking him in, I head to my room.

I don't know what time I fell asleep last night. But when I wake up the next morning, there's no denying the cold, empty space next to me. My nerves kick in again when I glance at the clock and it reads a quarter 'til ten. *Maybe he came in sometime during the morning and fell asleep in the spare room again.* Since everyone is still asleep, I tiptoe through the house to check for Xavien. But after a few minutes of searching, it becomes obvious that he isn't here. I call his cell, and again it goes straight to voicemail. All of sudden there's a loud knock at the door, causing my heart to race. I prayed it isn't the police with news that something had happened to my husband. Oddly enough, there's no one there when I finally make it to the door. Only a brown manila envelope. Carefully, I scan the yard to make sure there is no one waiting to take me by surprise. After the coast is clear, I pick up the envelope and step back inside.

I glance at the counter and notice it's identical to the envelope someone had given Xavien yesterday. A part of me just wants to throw it away, but when I turn it over, there's a message written in bold letters saying:

LOOK INSIDE TO KNOW THE TRUTH

With trembling hands, I undo the clasp of the envelope. When I pull out the contents on the inside, I feel as if a part of me has died. For a minute I forget how to breathe. I'm just frozen in time, staring at the pictures of Xavien and Marianna. And each one feels like a knife being driven into my heart, slowly cutting out whatever dreams I had for us in the future. My heart still refuses to believe that Xavien would do this to me. But with one picture of them sitting in a booth together, another with them standing with her arms around him, and the last with… Marianna on his lap kissing him, was all the confirmation I needed that my husband, the father of my child, has cheated on me. I run to the nearest bathroom and throw up. *How could he do this to me? How could he do this to our family?* After my divorce was final from Jaylen, I promised myself that I would never go through this shit again. But here I am going through the same shit with another no good nigga. I'm not going to sit around waiting for him to come home and throw divorce papers in my face. Or brag about how much better Marianna is than me. I dry my tears and go upstairs to pack my shit.

About an hour later, I'm rolling my suitcase down to the living room. I must have been making a lot of noise because Ty comes running in to check on things. He pauses when he sees me with my suitcase.

"Morning Ma. You good?"

"I'm fine. Can you do me a favor and get that bag out of X's room? When you're finished, I'm going to need you to get him dressed for me."

"Ma, what's going on? Why you leaving?"

I feel myself about to break down again. "Ty just…please do that for me, okay?"

His hazel eyes are filled with concern as he stares at me. He eventually nods. "Aight."

I'd just made it to the front door when I hear the lock turn and Xavien walks in.

"Baby, we need to…" He pauses when he notices my suitcase.

"Ray, what you doing?"

I ignore his question and walk back towards the stairs.

"Ray, I need to holla at you about something."

"What the fuck do you want, X?!"

He stands there for a second, probably surprised that I came at him that way. "Ray, you need to chill with that tone, you feel me. I got some shit to tell you."

"Oh, now you want to talk. Now you got some fucking time to talk to me. How about you tell me where the fuck you been all night? Explain that shit. We get into one muthafuckin' argument and you can't bring your punk ass home!"

Xavien takes a deep breath. I can tell he's trying to keep his composure. "Ray, after that bullshit popped off, I went to get a drink. I got fucked up. Couldn't drive so, I went to the office. That's where the fuck I been aight."

I shake my head as I go to the couch and pick up the pictures. "Like you told me yesterday, explain this bullshit then." I throw the pictures at him.

"That's a bunch of bullshit! I ain't do shit with that bitch, Ray!"

"Just stop! Stop! Stop! For once in your life stop fucking lying to me! I believed you when you said you would never…God, I believed you…"

As hard as I try, I couldn't hold back my tears anymore. This shit hurts too much. Heartache is nothing new to me. But for the first time, I thought I finally had something real. I'm glad I found out it was all bullshit. Xavien tries to comfort me, but I shove him away.

"Don't you dare fucking touch me. How could you do this to me? After sitting there and listening to everything I've been through? How could you hurt me?"

"Baby…I love you. I would never do no shit like that."

With him being this close to me there was no denying the smell of alcohol on him or that bitch's perfume. When I finally take a closer look, I can see lipstick and makeup all over his shirt.

"Then how the fuck did her perfume and makeup get all over you, X?"

He sighs heavily. "Baby, you wouldn't believe me if I told you. But I promise I ain't do shit with her."

I shake my head as I pull off my beautiful, platinum wedding ring and throw it at him. "You're right, I don't believe you. Just like you didn't believe me. As far as I'm concerned, you can have that bitch. My son and I are leaving."

Xavien shakes his head. "Nah Ray, don't do this shit."

"You did it! This is your fucking fault! You let shit get to this point!"

I don't know when Ty and Ms. Lana came into the room or how much they heard, but I was done with this conversation.

I walk over to Ty and take my son out of his arms along with his bag. Ty grabs my suitcase and follows me outside. When everything is loaded up I embrace him tightly.

"I'll be at my dad's house if you want to come live with us, but I won't be mad at you if you stay here."

"Ma, I don't understand what's going on with y'all."

I shake my head as I fight back tears. "Me either."

"Hit me up when you make it there safe."

"I will." I then get in my car and back out of the driveway.

CHAPTER 16

Xavien

This shit did not just happen. I know damn well shit did not go down like that. For a minute, I'm just stuck. Waiting for somebody to wake my ass up from this fucked up nightmare. When I got up this morning, I thought this fucking hangover would be the worst thing I felt today. But coming home to find out my wife had packed her shit and was leaving my ass…I can't even lie, it feels like a fucking sledgehammer just hit me in the chest. I take a seat on the couch, resting my head in my hands as I try to process what the fuck just happened. True, I was lit last night after drinking too much, but I know damn well I ain't fuck around on my wife. I remember that bitch jumping on me. And cursing her dumb ass out for even offering me that raggedy ass pussy. But if you would have asked me how I got to my office, now that shit I can't tell you. All I can say is my big homie upstairs was watching out for my ass. When I did come to, I was stretched out on the couch. Had my work boots and everything else still on. My head was booming and there was this loud ass ringing in my ears. It took a minute for my dumbass to realize it was the damn phone. Thought I'd fell and fucked my head up for real.

"Verano," I answered when I finally make it to my desk.

"How'd you like those pictures of me and yo' wife nigga?" a dude asked me.

This fucked up headache didn't stop me from recognizing that it was the same muthafucka who's been playing on my phone for the past few weeks.

"Real funny muthafucka. The only reason you still breathin' is cause you wanna hide like a lil' bitch."

"I wasn't hidin' when I met up with yo' thick ass wife though. You ought to be more careful, Chains. Letting a fine ass bitch like that meet up with random niggas. It would've been too easy to finish what I started two years ago."

"The fuck you mean by that nigga?"

"Oh, she ain't tell you who I was did she? Knowing yo' ass you probably ain't give her a chance. I know you flipped out when them pictures hit yo' doorstep." His punk ass started laughing. "Don't worry big homie. I ain't smash yo' wifey. Not yet anyway. But I did grab a handful of that phat ass though."

I swear for God, I wished that muthafucka was in front of me talking that shit. The walls would've been dripping with that niggas blood. Yeah, he's talking tough over the phone about putting hands on my wife. But when I catch that nigga, he gonna regret the day he looked at her.

"I hope you enjoyed it nigga 'cause that's the last ass you ever gonna grab."

"You right, Chains. I did enjoy it. But not as much as I'm gonna enjoy what happens next. I hope you like that other delivery that was made to your house this morning. But I don't think wifey's gonna appreciate it too much though." Then his punk ass hung up.

While staring at those pictures on the floor, all I can do is shake my head. Them muthafuckas got me, real talk. Caught my ass slippin' and fucked up my ties with the one person who means the world to me. A soft hand rubs my back, causing me to lift my head and look into Mama Armateo's brown eyes. She wraps her thin arms around me, kinda like my mom used to do when shit was bothering me.

"Are you ok, son?" she asks.

I shake my head and lean back on the couch. "Nah. As fucked up as them pictures look, I ain't cheat on my wife, Ma."

She nods. "I believe you, Xavien. Anyone can see how much you love RayVen."

"Yeah, everybody but her."

"She only responded the same way you did with her yesterday. You were so filled with hurt and anger that you didn't even listen to what she had to say."

I sigh heavily as guilt starts to hit me again.

"You can't cry over spilled milk, son. What you have to do now is figure out a way to fix things."

I nod. "The only way I can do that is going back on my word. I promised you and the old man that I would leave my past in Jersey, but that shit tracked me down anyway."

"I remember that promise, but you also made a promise to your wife and son to protect them at all costs. Do what you have to do, my son. But be careful."

I nod and go upstairs to get funk of that bitch's stink ass perfume off me.

By the time I'm cleaned up and dressed, I make it downstairs in time to catch my phone going off. A small part of me wishes it was baby girl, but it was Carmine hitting me up instead.

"Wassup fam?" I answer.

"X, you good?" he asks.

"Just got home."

"Everything cool?

"Nah, some shit went down."

"Yeah, we figured some other shit might go down. We been keeping a close watch on your house since you left," he tells me. "So when that muthafucka dropped that package off at your front step this morning, we grabbed his ass."

Shit, that was the best news I've heard all day. "Word, where y'all at?"

"I'll text you the address."

"Aight, cool."

Soon as I hang up, I notice Ty coming back in the house. From the way this lil' nigga is mugging me, I honestly can't say how he's gonna come at me. Just hope it wouldn't come to me dropping his lil' ass. Even though I get why he's probably pissed at me. We stand in the middle of the living room, staring each other down for a minute.

"X, I'ma need you to keep it a hunnid with me, real talk," he says. "Did you fuck around on my mama?"

"Nah fam. True, them muthafuckas caught me slippin', but not enough do wifey foul, you feel me."

He stares at me for a minute but finally nods. "What you need me to do?"

"Look out for mom dukes 'til we get back. I'll put you on soon as I know something."

"Aight, I got you."

The address Carmine hit me with is about 30 minutes away from the house. I end up riding through this fucked up neighborhood filled with abandoned buildings, homeless people, and dope fiends. The GPS leads me all the way down an alley, where I eventually see two hummers parked in front of an old warehouse. I recognize V.J.'s truck off the bat, so I know I'm in the right spot. After texting them that I made it, one of the crew meets me out front to show me where they at. The inside of the building smells like somebody poured a gallon of piss and shit on the floor. Most of the doors on the inside are rusted over from not being used in years. I follow dude down a flight of stairs and hear rats running all over the place. This was the grimiest, most fucked up building I'd seen in a minute. Crazy as this might sound, I've been missing shit like this. I nod at my bros when I finally meet them at the bottom. They got some dude tied to a chair with a sackcloth over his head. V.J. tosses me a pair of gloves, then signals for one of the crew to remove the bag off dude's head.

He looks scared as fuck when he realizes we have his ass outnumbered. "Man, I ain't do shit!" he says. We ain't even touch his ass and he was already bitching. "Y'all might as well lemme go man."

I slide the gloves on my hands and swing on this lying muthafucka a few times. Carmine eventually has to pull me off him. Dude groans and spits some blood on the floor. I fall back just a little bit and allow Carmine to say what he needs to.

He squats down to get eye level with dude. "Real talk homie, you need to be real fucking careful about what you say to us right now. You see my brother over there…" Carmine nods in my direction, causing dude to look at me. "He ain't in a real good mood right now."

Dude shakes his head. "Chains, it wasn't my fault man. I just did what they paid me to do."

"Quit bitchin' muthafucka and tell me what you know."

He shakes his head as if tryna get his mind right. "It was Nolo, man. Everything that's been going down lately is cuz of him."

"That's the same name Ray mentioned," Carmine tells me. "Bro, who is that?"

I shake my head, not believing that punk ass muthafucka had enough balls to come at me on this level. "Some bitch ass nigga I got into it with in prison. I beat his ass when him and his homies tried to jump RayVen."

Dude nods. "He said one of his homies got bodied that night. That's why he had to clap back on you, because you fucked up his

146

whole operation."

V.J. swings on dude catching him in the stomach. "Shut the fuck up. Ain't nobody ask you shit."

"This shit doesn't make sense though. Nolo just a low-level nigga, and he damn sure ain't smart enough to pull all this off by himself," I tell them. "Who's helping that nigga?"

Dude is still coughing from when V.J. hit him, so he doesn't answer me right away. I bust him in the back of the head to get his attention.

"Answer me muthafucka."

"Ah...shit man!" He shakes his head again. "Marciano...he helped him set all this shit up."

"Marciano Barajas? The same muthafucka who was begging me to work for his ass?"

"He doesn't use his whole name, that's only to run his businesses. It's Marciano Barajas Vargas. Manolo is his nephew..."

"Keep talking, my man," Carmine tells him.

"Nolo never got over what happened on the inside, so he asked Marciano to help him out. He knew he couldn't clap while on the inside, so Marciano helped to break him out of prison. Nolo ended up killing the Warden or some shit. When they figured out where Chains was, they had eyes on him and his wife ever since." Dude starts coughing again but continues. "They needed somebody on the inside who could drive a wedge between you and your wife, so they got Marianna to get a job at your wife's job to start shit."

"Why her?"

"Cuz they know you and her have history; besides she'll do whatever it takes to help her father and cousin."

"I thought that bitch said her old man worked in Jersey."

Dude shakes his head. "That was her grandpa. Marciano is her real father. Manolo is her cousin. He knew she felt some type of way about what happened between y'all in the past. So, they got together to plot against you."

"How deep does this plot run?"

"Real deep. When Marianna got the job at the center, she was able to go into the files and get y'all information. Phone numbers, addresses, that kinda shit. She gave it to Nolo so he could start putting the calls in to your wife and sending her the flowers. I was there that day when Marciano came by your office to offer you the job. When you kicked him out, he told me to stay behind until you left. Then I was supposed to call Marianna to let her know so she could be on the side of the road when you came by to see your wife. They knew having her in your car would cause some drama between y'all. But when that didn't work, they made sure to have those flowers delivered that day when you and your wife went to lunch."

"What about those pictures you delivered? How'd they set all that up?" Carmine asks.

"I took them," he says. "I went to the farmer's market with Nolo when he met up with your wife. Once I got the ones I needed, I was able to print them off real quick and deliver them."

I punch him again just for the hell of it. "What about the ones you set me up with?"

"When I dropped the first set of pictures off, I waited a few blocks away until I saw you leave, then I followed you. Marianna wasn't too far away, so I called her and told her to meet me. When we saw you go into the bar, she went in to do what she had to do."

This shit was unbelievable. These muthafuckas ain't had nothing else better to do than to get together to try and fuck up my life. Damn, was the hate that real?

"So, what was this bullshit about Marciano offering me a job?"

He sighs in frustration. "The plan was get you to work for him after you and your wife split up. He knew that you would want to know who was behind all the shit that's been going on. So he was gonna offer to help you in exchange for putting in the work for him. After he got you to take out his competition, he was gonna set you up for Manolo to take you out."

"How we know this ain't a bunch of bullshit just to save your ass?" Carmine asks him.

"Man, I ain't lying. They probably gonna kill me anyway cuz I know too much. And they probably don't have much use for me anymore."

"Neither do we muthafucka." I pull out my gun and unload my clip on his ass.

A familiar feeling comes over me as I watch the nigga's body slump down in the chair. All of the bullshit that's been going on these past few weeks begins to hit me full force. The explosion at my job site, all the bullshit phone calls, the arguments between me and my wife. Now that I know who was behind all this bullshit, it only fueled the rage burning beneath my skin. Had me feeling like Dr. Jekyll or some shit, except I ain't need no magic potion to bring the savage out of me. I'd let this crazy muthafucka sleep for too long, and it felt good as fuck to finally let him out again. The worst mistake these muthafuckas made was thinking I went soft because I went legit. Chains ain't never left muthafucka; I just been sleep. My brothers must've recognized the look in my eyes 'cause both of them had a smile on their face.

"As soon as we get enough background on Marciano, we can follow the script ole boy put us onto," Carmine tells me. "Get you working for him and then gut that muthafucka from the inside out."

"Cool..." I say with a nod. "It's about time I remind these muthafuckas who the fuck Chains is."

CHAPTER 17

RayVen

The sound of X laughing outside causes me to get up from the couch and look out the back window for the third time. He and Xavien were in my dad's back yard playing their version of one-on-one. I can't help laughing as X tries to dribble the basketball that's almost as big as he is. Xavien picks him up to help him shoot the ball in the hole. He starts cheering like he just scored the game winning point. It's been a few weeks since we came to live with my dad, and I still haven't made up my mind about what I'm going to do yet. My head and my heart are on two opposite sides of the spectrum. That day when I packed my bags to leave, you couldn't tell me I wasn't through with Xavien Verano. When I pulled up in Dad's driveway, he was outside doing yardwork. Chile, I jumped out the car all mad, got my baby out the car seat, and strut through the front door without saying a word.

"So, you're just going to kick in my front door without saying hello?" my dad asked jokingly.

"Dad, I'm sorry but I am done with that man, you hear me."

"Uh huh," he said with a nod. "Do you want to talk about it?"

"Nope, I sure don't."

Since X had dozed off, I put him on the couch and covered him up so I can go get our bags.

"Well pick a room, baby girl," he said.

Shoot, he didn't have to tell me twice. Dad already has a room setup for X just in case I ever need him to babysit, so I'm good on that part. But I'd always liked his master bedroom which he never uses. No matter how much wealth he's accumulated, Dad still isn't hard to please. He prefers to sleep in the room downstairs that's closer to the kitchen. That way he can sneak and get his usual snack of double stuffed Oreos. But anyway, I set up camp in the master bedroom and didn't have any problems with my decision. By the time I fell asleep that night, I'd convinced myself I didn't want or need my husband. That is…until the next afternoon when Xavien came by to see X. When the doorbell rang, I sauntered to the front door, attitude fully cocked, with my best game face on. Honey, when I snatched the door open to see him standing there with that black polo shirt, jeans, fresh braids in his hair, and smelling all good, I forgot why the hell I was mad in the first place. Suddenly I felt self-conscious in my t-shirt and leggings. We kind of stared at each other for a while. I guess neither one of us knew what to say. But from the way he was eyeing me and licking his lips, I knew that he missed me. I can't lie, I was looking at his lips the whole time; fantasizing about what he could do with his mouth. He knew he was wrong for that; probably was doing that shit on purpose.

"DADDY!!" X screamed from behind me and came running to Xavien.

He scooped him up in his arms. "How you been doing, lil' homie?"

"Terrible. I missed you," X told him, and my heart broke.

"I missed you too, homie." I started to close the door so they can enjoy their time together. "Ray…"

Dammit why did he have to say my name like that?

"Is it cool with you if I take him to the park?"

I only nodded.

I appreciated him asking me for permission, although he doesn't need to. No matter what is going on between us, I would never keep him from seeing his son. And believe me, he's been here every day. EVERY.DAMN.DAY. Walking by me with that damn cologne on. Getting on my god damn nerves. Absently, I touch my ring finger. My left hand feels naked without my wedding ring. I put on a brave face for my son, but late at night I cry because I feel like I've lost my best friend. The two years I've had with Xavien have been the best years of my life by far, and now it's all over.

X starts squealing again and I see Xavien holding him up in the air; pretending like he's flying. Then they both crash and take a seat on the ground.

Look at him, he swears he's cute. I roll my eyes at Xavien through the window. Resenting the fact that he can make a red t-shirt and jeans look so damn good. I hate that every time he comes by I always end up lurking at the window. But I can't seem to stop myself from watching him. Like I don't have a ton of files on my laptop to tend to. In a way, this kind of reminds me of the time when I was first debating on whether

I should take Xavien on as a client. My supervisor at the time, and the Warden, thought it would be a good idea for me to do some observation on him while he was working out. I had my pen and notebook ready to jot down my notes like I normally would. But honey…when Xavien took off his shirt and the sun started beaming on him like a spotlight causing him to sweat, my mind was everywhere else but taking notes. That fantasy got so good I had to go to the restroom and take my panties off because they'd gotten so wet. And trust me, not much has changed.

"When are you going to stop spying on the man and go talk to him?" my dad asks, scaring the shit out of me.

"Dad…you scared me. How long have you been standing there?" I put a hand on my chest trying to relax my rapidly beating heart.

"Long enough to know you need to be outside talking to your husband."

I suck my teeth. "Oh please, I'm just watching X."

"Mm hmm…like you do every time he comes by."

"Ugh…I mean Xavier…your grandson." I love my dad but he is working my last nerve; mainly because he's right.

Dad laughs and shakes his head at me. "I swear you're as stubborn as your mother used to be. You and I both know Xavien will go through hell and back to protect his son…and his hard-headed wife."

I roll my eyes because he was right about that too. "That's good to know."

Dad surprises me by pulling out a chair for me at the kitchen table.

"Come sit down, baby girl. Let's talk for a minute."

I shake my head in defiance. There is no way I'm having this conversation with my father. "Look Dad, I appreciate it, but I really don't—"

"RayVen Cheyenne, bring your hard-headed behind over here and sit down!"

I cross my arms in front of my chest and stomp over to the chair. He's lucky he's my dad because I swear I'd chop him in the throat for raising his voice at me.

"Thank you," he says and takes a seat across from me. "Take it from someone who's been married for thirty plus years. Just because you hit a bump in the road, that doesn't mean you abandon the car and walk. Times have changed, but marriage has been and always will be a full-time job. But when you share it with the right person, it makes putting in that time worthwhile."

I sigh but don't say anything.

"Now, I'm not going to get involved in your marriage. Whatever issues you all are dealing with, it's up to you two to fix it. But you don't see how that man looks at you when you're giving him your behind to kiss. He's hurting just as much as you are."

I shake my head in disbelief. "You always take his side...I didn't make him cheat on me...he did that all on his own."

"RayVen, I'm not taking sides. But one thing I do know, is for someone to love you as much as Xavien does, he wouldn't be able to look his son in the eye if he did anything to hurt his mother. True, he may have let his guard down and done something stupid, like we all do at some time or another. But I doubt things went that far. He's not Jaylen, baby girl. So, don't make him pay for his mistakes."

I felt myself getting emotional again. "I'm going to run to take a shower. Keep an eye on X until I'm finished please."

While in the shower I shed tears of frustration, because deep down I know what my father said made sense. To an extent. I think he was just being optimistic about our situation. No matter how pissed off I am, I still love Xavien. But I can't bring myself to talk to him just yet. At the end of the day, he still doubted me and accused me of cheating on him. And he let himself be caught in a precarious position with Marianna. He should have fucking known better. I get out the shower in time to see Xavien carrying X into his room. The first night or two away from home X slept just fine. But we've been gone so long that I think he's starting to sense something is up. Now, he won't fall asleep unless both of us are in the room with him. I tighten my robe around my waist and take a deep breath. When I am sure I've gathered enough nerves to be around Xavien, only then do I go to my son's room.

While Xavien is giving him a bath, I go ahead and get his pajamas ready. I take them into the bathroom and sit them on the counter.

"Hey Mommy," X says with a smile.

"Hey sweet pea." I feel Xavien's eyes on me as I go back in the room to turn his bed down.

A few minutes later, X struts out of the bathroom in his PJs. "I'm ready!"

I start laughing. "For what short stuff?"

"To dance." He starts doing these little moves he saw on a cartoon earlier, causing us to laugh.

"How about you dance your lil' behind in the bed," Xavien tells him.

X starts laughing when Xavien picks him up and carries him over to the crib.

"Daddy, you leaving now?"

Xavien nods. "Yeah, but I'll be back to see you tomorrow."

"Stay, please Daddy. Please." X tightens his grip on Xavien's neck.

Seeing how much X misses his father caused a wave of guilt to sweep over me.

"Didn't I tell you earlier I ain't going nowhere?" he asks him.

X sniffles as he fights back tears but manages to nod.

"Aight then, no matter what happens, I'm gonna always be here for you."

"Okay, Daddy." He hugs Xavien again. "Mommy come."

I walk over and give X a big hug before putting him to bed. Xavien and I sit in silence as we watch him close his eyes. It doesn't take long before he settles down and starts snoring.

"Thank you for letting me come by and see him, Ray," Xavien tells me. "I appreciate that."

I shake my head. "You don't have to thank me. He's as much your child as he is mine. And what kind of mother would I be if I kept the two of you apart? At the end of the day we all would suffer. But I appreciate you coming by the way you have." I look up to notice him staring at me. "What?"

He smiles a little. "That's the most you've said to me in two weeks. Just good to hear your voice, that's all."

I wave him on in an attempt to fight back a smile. "I'll walk you out."

He nods. "Aight."

I try not to get lost in his cologne as I walk him to the front door. *Just let him out and lock the door,* I tell myself over and over again.

"Have a good night, okay." I twist the handle and hold the door open for him.

"You too." Xavien turns to leave but pauses. "You been getting any more calls at your job."

I shake my head. "Nothing yet. Hopefully he's learned his lesson."

Xavien nods. "Believe me he will."

Something about the way he said that made me nervous.

"By the way, there's something in the kitchen for you," he tells me and walks towards his car.

"Xavien…" He turns to face me. "Be careful okay."

It may have been dark outside but I couldn't miss that smirk on his face. I linger in the doorway long enough to watch him drive off down the road. *Go inside and lock the door RayVen,* I scold myself and go back in the house. Instead of going upstairs, I walk in the kitchen to see what is waiting for me. On the counter is a big, beautiful bouquet of pink and white roses.

This dude. I can only shake my head as I pick up the card that came with it.

I know you ain't thought I was gonna give up on you that easy.

At the end of the day I love you and you still

My wife. I'm going to war to get you back by my side, baby.

No matter what happens, know that you got my heart

And nobody can take your place in mine.

Love Always,

X

For the first time in two weeks, I allow myself to smile. I carefully grab the vase of flowers and take them up to my room.

CHAPTER 18

Xavien

$\mathcal{S}$ ince I'm on the way to Harland's crib to drop X off, I thought it would be a good idea to holla at him man to man. Me and him been cool since that night in the hospital. And even though he ain't acting any different towards me, I wanted to put him on to the shit that's been going on between me and RayVen. The last thing I want is for dude to think that I'd played his daughter. Speaking of which, a day hasn't gone by where I haven't been thinking about her. Shit, I miss my baby. I hate rolling over in the middle of the night and not feeling that fluffy ass in my stomach. Or not being able to check on lil' dude when I wake up in the middle of the night. The house ain't been the same since they left. Which is why I made it my business to come by here every day. RayVen still being kinda cold towards me. But it's all good. As long as I'm able to lay eyes on her and X, I'm cool. She is starting to talk to me a little more when I come through though. I guess those flowers I left in the house the other night knocked a little bit of that ice from her heart.

With all the shit that's been going on, I admit I been slacking with the romantic shit. That bubble bath I gave her was the first time I did something like that for her in a minute. Before we had X, I used to do shit like that for her all the time. Then when that muthafucka started sending her flowers and shit, I kinda had to check myself. After all this bullshit is done, I'ma make sure I do all I can to make my wife feel special.

But Ray thinks she's slick though. I peeped her ass out for a while now. Coming to the door to get X with them damn leggings on. Knowing damn well my eyes gonna be all over them thick ass thighs. For a minute, I thought it was just a coincidence. But all week she been wearing some tight ass pants, so I know she tryna tease me with that phatty. Knowing I can't get in them guts like I want to. Since she wanna do me like that, I make sure every time I come through I'm swagged out. The icing on the cake is that cologne that makes her cookie wet. Two can definitely play at this shit. But I play to win.

"Xavien, how are you doing son?" Harland asks.

Once X is situated in the house, he walks out to the car to help make sure I got everything.

"Not complaining," I tell him. "You gotta minute? I need to holla at you about something."

"Yeah, I'm not doing anything but watching reruns." He leans against the hood of my car. "Hard head still giving you a hard time?"

I laugh a little bit. "Ray wouldn't be who she is if she didn't."

This time he laughs.

"But on some real shit, I just wanted to let you know that I ain't fuck around on your daughter."

AYE STORM

He only nods.

"When you gave me your permission to marry her, I gave you my word that I'll do all I can to keep her safe. And that's some shit I refuse to go back on."

Harland looks at me then. "You in some kinda trouble, X?"

"Some dude I got into with on the inside been coming at us." I reach inside the passenger window and grab the pictures off the seat.

"Is this him with RayVen?" he asks as he looks through them.

"Yeah, at the time I ain't know that she met up with him until after the fact. But she went out there to try and squash shit."

Harland shakes his head. "What if this asshole had tried something or wasn't alone? Didn't she know anything could have happened to her?"

"That's exactly the same shit that was going through my head."

"So, where is he?"

"Now that, I haven't figured out yet. His punk ass has been hiding behind his uncle. Dude gotta little bit of pull and has been helping him play on our phone and shit."

He nods. "You have a name on this Uncle? Maybe I can check into things and see who we're dealing with."

I knew there was a reason why I fucks with Harland. He's a straight up G and don't even know it. "Marciano Barajas."

"There isn't a business owner in Atlanta who hasn't heard that name. Some say he's a loan shark. He tries to trick people, saying he'll invest in their business, claiming he'll market their services to raise their clientele. Soon as business picks up, he comes to take his percentage…with interest."

I nod. "Sounds like you've had a run in with him."

"Nah, just the fools who were dumb enough to sell their souls for a profit. A few of them have come by my office trying to see if they can cash in any of their stocks to pay him back."

"Think you can get a list of them places that he's rolling deep with?"

He nods. "Yeah, I can do that for you. You going to be alright going against him and his goons alone?"

I nod. "I'll be cool, but I ain't alone."

The sound of tires grab my attention and I see a Hummer creeping by the house. With RayVen and X being over here, I told a few of our crew to roll by so they can know where to be. The front window rolls down and I nod at the driver, letting him know everything is cool. He nods back and keeps it moving.

"There's eyes on y'all now just in case things go south, you feel me."

He nods. "Appreciate that. Watch out for yourself X."

I glance at the front window to see RayVen peeking through the curtains. Nosey ass. I wave at her so she knows I see, and she snatches the curtain closed.

Me and Harland just shake our heads.

"I'll make sure those two are taken care of. Just handle your business, son."

TAYE STORM

"No doubt." I shake his hand before hopping in my ride and driving off.

After Harland hit me back with the list I asked for, I was ready to get down to business. My bros have been doing heavy surveillance on Marciano while I was making sure my family was situated. Apparently, he is scheduled to have a meeting with a few of the business owners that were still refusing to pay the increase he wanted. From what we figured out about Marciano, he will do anything to keep his grimy ass moves out of the public eye. That's why he was holding this meeting after midnight. I roll up a few minutes after twelve and scope out five or six cars chilling in the parking lot of a restaurant. The only security I see are the men in black looking niggas posted up outside of Marciano's Expedition. Either the other dudes are inside or he's not rolling that deep tonight. I climb out of V.J.'s Hummer and they peel off down the road. It crosses my mind to watch how I move when approaching the door. But the two muthafuckas who are supposed to be keeping an eye on shit are playing on their phones. Sloppy asses. They didn't see me until I was right on them. But by then I'd knocked both of their asses out. Don't get me wrong, I had no issues about bodying the muthafuckas, but that ain't a part of the script right now.

Once I'm inside the building, I walk to the back room where everyone is sitting. The inside is dark except for that one room, which looks like some kinda private dining area. So, they had no idea that I'm even here. For a minute, I just kick back and listen to their conversation.

"Mr. Barajas, when I signed the deed of my restaurant over to you, I thought that would have covered the balance of what I owe you," one dude says. "With the business that's been coming to this place, I'm sure you've made back what I owe you many times over. So, I don't understand why I have to keep paying you."

Marciano only smirks at him. "I understand your frustration, Michael. Really, I do. But like I tell all of my clients, you have to read the fine print. The designated interest must be paid before you're free and clear."

"And how are our families supposed to live?" someone else asks. "Do you know I'm having to pull from my kids' college fund just to keep our heat on?"

I was tired of listening to this bullshit. "Either freeze or let they ass flip burgers muthafucka."

All eyes turn in my direction. I am close enough so they can know where I am, but there is enough darkness shielding me so they can't see my face. Yeah, I'm definitely on some gangsta shit tonight.

"And just who the hell are you?" a dude in a business suit asks.

"Trust me, the less you know about me, the better muthafucka." Everyone in the room looks scared as fuck, even Marciano's dumb ass.

"Oh yeah," dude in the suit says. "Quit hiding in the dark and …"

I unload my clip three times catching his ass in the chest. The other dudes jump out their seats at the sight of their partner bloody and bleeding on the floor.

"Any of you other muthafuckas got shit to say?" I ask them.

They all shake their heads.

"Now that we got that bullshit out way. Either pay what you owe, or I'm coming to your crib to draw blood from everybody in that muthafucka, you feel me."

I fire off a few shots and they take off out the back door. Soon as everybody hauled ass, Marciano starts clapping. I step out in full view as I remove the hood from my head.

"Now that was fucking impressive!" he tells me. "Wasn't expecting to see you so soon, Chains."

"Life has taught me to expect the unexpected, you feel me?"

He nods. "I definitely feel you. So, I guess this means you'll be taking me up on my offer."

I shrug. "More or less. But I don't work for free."

"After seeing the way you just handled those assholes, just name your price." He looks at the dude lying dead on the floor and laughs.

"We'll settle that a little later." I toss the picture of Nolo and RayVen on the table. "Who's the muthafucka in this picture?"

He gets this cocky smirk on his face. "Well, I don't know, Chains. Did you ask your wife? She looks a little cozy with him to me."

I point the barrel of the gun at his head which is still smoking. "Don't fuck with me muthafucka. This nigga been fucking with her, and I need to know who he is."

He nods. "I'm sorry that was in poor taste, Chains. I know a lot of people all over the city, so I'm sure we can track this guy down."

"Is that right? Well, if you can deliver like you say, then I don't have an issue with putting in some work for you."

He gets this big ass grin on his face. "Sounds like a deal. And I'm a man of my word. I'll start looking for someone to handle that construction business for you."

I shake my head. "Nah, I can handle my own business. Don't wanna give muthafuckas a reason to get suspicious."

He nods again. "You're absolutely right. Besides, I have an image to uphold in the city, and I don't want to tarnish that until I get the status I need."

This is one simple minded muthafucka. "Just deliver that muthafucka in the picture with my wife, then we'll be even, comprende?"

"Claro." He extends his hand to me, and I had to fight the urge to put a bullet in that muthafucka. But I eventually shake it. "If you have a few minutes, I'd like to go over business with you so there won't be any misunderstanding."

I kick the dead dude out the way and pull up a chair. "I'm listening."

"There are three targets I have in mind, all of which are high-standing citizens of the community. So, I'm willing to compensate you with $100 grand for each one that can be persuaded in my favor."

I only nod.

"After I have the third individual under contract, I'm sure we will have discovered who's been stalking your wife. Once we locate him, I can more than likely arrange for the two of you to have a "confrontation" somewhere private, just in case things get a little heated."

I smirk at him. "Cool."

"How do you want me to get in touch with you when I find this guy?"

"Have him call me when he's ready to square up," I tell him.

By the time I exit the building, Marciano's bullshit security is just beginning to come to. I kick one of the muthafuckas in the face as I walk by, knocking him out again. He only needs one to drive him home. I walk a few blocks until I see V.J.'s Hummer waiting on me. They pull up to meet me and I hop in the back.

CHAPTER 19

$\mathcal{I}$ should've known. I should have known. As soon as I saw Dad and Xavien talking the other day, I should have known those two were up to something. With it being Sunday, I thought I'd get an early start on dinner. I honestly could have slept in, because I only had to cook enough for Dad, me, and the little munchkin. But I guess old habits die hard. I would've been doing the same thing if I was… Anyway, I had my mind all set to clean and season enough chicken for two and a half people. But when I go into the kitchen, Dad has three more packs on the counter, along with six or seven bags full of groceries.

"Dad, who in the hell is all this food for?" I ask confused.

He shrugs innocently. "It's been a little while since we've had a big family dinner so I invited some people over."

"Oh really?" I ask suspiciously. "Like who?"

"Just a few friends of mine."

I didn't think much of it until I see him pulling out his XL deep fryer and a five-gallon jug of cooking oil.

"Are you sure we're not feeding an army?" I joke.

"Girl, quit asking so many questions and clean that chicken."

"Fine." I can only shake my head.

About an hour or so later I have all the chicken cleaned, seasoned, and ready for the deep fryer. All of a sudden, the doorbell rings. Since I didn't see Dad anywhere, I start washing my hands so I can answer the door.

"Go ahead and drop the chicken; I'll get it," Dad says rushing pass me.

What the hell is this man up to?

The grease starts popping and crackling as I stack each piece into the basket. As soon as I lower the basket into the grease, I hear X scream.

"Daddy!"

I turn around to see Xavien picking him up as he walks into the house. *No, he didn't. I just know Dad did not!* Next thing I know, Ms. Lana is walking through the door with a hand full of containers. From the smell of things, she's brought desserts. Then I see Ty, Carmine, and V.J. following close behind her. I am so done with all of them. But I have to admit I'm glad to see everyone. While all the men situate themselves in front of Dad's 55-inch TV to watch football, Ms. Lana joins me in the kitchen.

"Hope you don't mind a little help," she tells me.

"I need all the help I can get to feed that crew," I laugh.

She gives me a big hug and a kiss on the cheek. "Good to see you, dear. I missed you."

"Same here."

After slaving and sweating over that hot ass stove for the next few hours, Ms. Lana and I have the fried chicken, mashed potatoes and gravy, and cornbread on the table. While she's warming up the apple pies and peach cobbler, I run upstairs to take a quick shower. Halfway down the hall I see Xavien coming out of the restroom. This is one of those rare times that he has his hair unbraided. It's pulled back into a thick ponytail which looks so good with his button down shirt and jeans. Damn him!

I must have been staring at him because he pauses. "You aight?" he asks with a smirk.

I clear my throat, "Oh…yeah sure, I'm fine; couldn't be better."

He nods. "See you downstairs." He brushes my cheek with his forefinger as he walks by me.

"What, did I have flour on my face?" I ask.

"Nah," he calls over his shoulder and keeps walking towards the stairs.

This nigga. I shake my head again as I head to the shower.

When I finally make it back downstairs, I have on a grey wrap dress that hugs my body in all the right places. Along with a pair of platinum dangling earrings and the matching necklace that rests between my breasts. If Xavien wanted to play that game, I can play it better.

"Wow…Mommy pretty!" X exclaims, causing everyone to turn

in my direction.

"I'll say," Dad says. "What's the occasion?"

I only shrug. "No occasion, just felt like putting on something different today." I glance over at Xavien who is staring at me and licking his lips. "Everyone ready to eat?"

"Starving," Xavien tells me.

I pick up X and switch my hips towards the dining room. Although I was a little nervous about how this day was going to turn out, we end up having a beautiful dinner. After Dad blesses the food, we were able to really enjoy ourselves. Especially with X sitting in his own little chair with his own food. We all laugh and joke just like we used to do. And for once I'm not stressing about all the bullshit that's been going on as of late. Even though every time I look up I notice Xavien looking across the table at me.

"Damn Ma, this chicken is blazing!" Ty tells me.

He and Xavien are neck and neck with three pieces under their belts already. And neither one of them seem to be coming up for air anytime soon.

"Can you even taste it?" I laugh. "You're eating it so fast."

He only laughs.

"Mommy, more chicken," X says while holding up his plate. I swear this little boy has an appetite just like his father.

I grab the tongs to give him a drum stick. "Anyone else want some more chicken?" I ask. How about all them greedy mofos hold up their plates, causing everyone to burst out laughing.

"I may as well get the rest out the kitchen." I get up from the table, causing Xavien to do the same.

"Hold up, lemme help you with that," he says, following me into the kitchen

"Oh…ok sure."

"Mm hmm…" Dad says loudly, causing everyone else to laugh again.

I shoot him a dirty look in response. *Always got something smart to say.*

Since I'm holding the dinner tray for the rest of the food, Xavien gets the hot pans out of the oven for me. *Keep it together, girl,* I tell myself. Now I know how R. Kelly was feeling in that one song. Because my mind is saying one thing but my body is definitely saying something else. Xavien doesn't have to touch me to bring me over the edge. And he knows this. All he has to do is give me that one look. Which is the same damn look he's been giving me all afternoon. I'll admit, I've been dickmatized since that first time. And no matter how mad I am, it still doesn't change things. I put a little space between us so I can fill up the tray with more food. His fingers lightly caress my arm, sending a warm shiver through my body. *Leave me alone demon!* I swear I wish I had some holy water or something.

"I'm loving that dress on you," Xavien says finally.

I fight the blush that is trying to make its way to my face. "Thank you."

"Welcome."

Has his voice always been so deep? It reminds me of a deep roll of thunder at the beginning of a storm. The heat from his eyes feels like a lightning bolt sending a thousand volts of electricity through my body.

Don't look in his eyes. Just focus on what you're doing. "By the way, thank you for the flowers and the card. They were really beautiful."

"Ain't no need to thank me for that."

I only nod. *RayVen, finish grabbing the damn chicken!*

"Ray…"

"Yes?"

Xavien gently removes the tray from my hand and turns me around to face him. "Look at me."

I focus my attention on a button in the middle of his shirt, until he lifts my chin with the back of his hand.

Don't do it! Don't do it! Before I can catch myself, I'm staring into those beautiful green eyes of his. *DAMN!*

He leans down softly, brushing his lips against mine before deepening the kiss. I don't resist when his tongue begins to make love to my throat. Or when his hands roam over my behind like they're trying to memorize the curve of my hips. *Bitch, ain't you supposed to be mad at his ass?* No matter how good it feels, my memory starts to remind me of those pictures of him with Marianna. And how he pushed me away when I tried talking to him. I place my hand on his shoulder. Taking my silent cue to stop, he reluctantly pulls back.

"Xavien…I need…" *Some dick!!!!*

He nods. "I know." He caresses the side of my face. "When you ready, get at me."

He then grabs the tray of food and takes it back into the dining room.

Damn him! Damn him! Damn him! Why did he have to kiss me like that? Xavien knows damn well I can't say no to him when he does that shit. Sneaky muthafucka. I lean against the kitchen counter for balance as I try to stop my legs from shaking.

"By the way Ma, the school gave me this paperwork they want you to look over," Ty tells me when I eventually make it back into the dining room.

I take a seat next to him when he reaches into his bag to get the forms. A part of me is a little nervous when he hands me this big white envelope with his name on it. I still remember what happened the last time I opened an envelope. And I'm still feeling the outcome of that shit. After taking a deep breath, I undo the clasp. When I pull out the stack of information, I notice the first page is an official letter of some kind.

Dear TySean Evans:

Congratulations! We are pleased to inform you that you have been accepted for admission to Georgia State University for the fall semester....

I let out a scream as I jump up to give him a hug. "Why didn't you tell me you applied to college?"

Ty starts blushing. "I wanted to surprise y'all."

"Oh my god, I'm so proud of you!"

Everyone starts clapping and congratulating him. "Man, y'all cut that shit out. Making a nigga blush and shit. But real talk, I couldn't have done it without y'all supporting me. So, I'm gonna need y'all to be front and center for graduation."

I glance over at Xavien who is staring at me. "Well, we'll definitely be there," I reassure him.

After a few more minutes of stuffing ourselves, everyone goes to relax. Dad and Ms. Lana take X into the living room with them while the men head outside.

"Ma, is it cool if I spend the night over here for a few?" Ty asks. "I need your help with filling out all these forms for my classes."

"Of course."

"Aight, be right back."

He takes off out the front door as I go to get started on the dishes. From the window I can see Ty talking to Xavien and his brothers. With all the nodding and hand gesturing between them, I figure they were plotting on something else. If I didn't know any better, I'd say Xavien asked Ty to spend the night so he can keep an eye on me. The loud engine of Ty's Camaro revs up and I watch as he carefully backs into the street. With him safely on his way I can put my focus back on the dishes. Then all of a sudden, I hear the gut wrenching sound of tires screeching and the sickening echo of two cars colliding.

"FUCK!" I hear Xavien scream as he takes off down the road with Carmine and V.J. following close behind him.

"Oh my god...Ty!"

The dishes crash into the sink when I run out of the kitchen and through the front door. When I make it up the street towards the intersection, all I can see is the red bumper of Ty's Camaro along with a bunch of shattered glass.

"Oh my god! Oh my god!"

I keep running until I see everyone in a nearby field. The closer I get, the more I'm able to see that the Camaro is flipped upside down with the wheels still spinning. One side of the car is so horribly mangled that I can't tell if it's the passenger side or the driver's side. My heart is beating so fast I'm afraid it's going to jump out of my chest. When I finally reach Xavien, he grabs me so I wouldn't see the carnage. But it is too late. Through the broken glass of the windshield, I can see Ty still in the driver's seat. His eyes are closed and his sweet face is covered in blood.

"NOOOO! PLEASE GOD! NO!" I scream. My knees give out from under me and Xavien scoops me up in his arms.

Through my tears I'm able to see the distant lights of the police as they approach. They were immediately followed by firemen and a paramedic. With the car being completely totaled, they had to cut Ty out of the car. As soon as they were able to get him loaded onto the stretcher, they rush him off to the hospital. Somehow, I manage to walk back to the house. I jump in the passenger seat of Xavien's car, and we speed out of the yard to catch the ambulance.

CHAPTER 20

Xavien

Here we go again, back in the muthafuckin' hospital.

To keep myself from pacing back and forth, I take a seat next to my baby and wrap my arm around her. She's still shaken up after what went down with Ty. I'm just glad that she finally stopped crying. Me… I'm more pissed off than anything else. A few minutes after we made it to the hospital, the police showed up wanting to ask us questions. Ty being hit was no accident, but a fuckin' hit and run. So, of course they wanted to know what we saw. But I ain't nowhere near in the mood to be answering a bunch of dumb ass questions from them. I ain't never fucked with the police and I ain't gonna start now. Since Carmine is a little more level headed than I am, I asked him to handle that shit for us. I shake my head as the events from earlier keep replaying in my mind. I swear that shit was like some crazy ass scene from a movie. After getting a stomach full of that blazing ass dinner, me and my bros went outside so we could get our crew on point to take down Marciano and Nolo. There have been way too many fuck ups without Tony and Enzo on our team. We all agreed that them half ass muthafuckas on our security had to go. So, we hit them up and told them to meet up with us with the quickness. As luck would have it, they were close enough where they could touch down in ATL within the next few hours. V.J. was on the phone giving them the address when Ty came out to holla at us.

"Yo X, I'ma run to the crib right quick," he told me. "Gotta get some gear so I can chill ova here with Ma for a few."

"Aight, hit us up if you need anything."

"Bet. I'll be right back," he said.

After he backed out of the yard, we started going over the best way to hit them niggas when our backup arrived. For some reason, the sound of an engine revving up caught my attention. By the time I looked up the street, an old school Chevy truck came flying through the intersection and slammed into the passenger side of Ty's car.

"FUCK!"

All of us took off running down the street to see about Ty. We made it around the corner in time to see his car flip over. But the muthafucka who hit him just kept on riding. Since there was a bunch of nosey muthafuckas just standing around with their mouth open, I yelled for one of them to call 911. As fucked up as the car was, the only thing that crossed my mind is getting him out before that shit caught fire. I swear I couldn't take seeing that shit today. We were trying to figure out the best way to pull him from the car before the paramedics came, when I heard RayVen screaming. I didn't want her to see how bad lil' dude was hurt so I hugged her close to me. While I was focused on trying to keep my wife from losing her damn mind, I told my brothers to make sure no dumb muthafuckas tried anything. By that time, the paramedics and everything was just pulling up. They pulled out a machine to cut the driver door off the car. When that was out the way, they put a neck brace on him and loaded him on the stretcher. I ain't gone lie, that shit hit me in the chest to see lil' dude like that. There was so much blood on him; we could barely see his face. I'm praying he pulls through all right.

"Is there family here for TySean Evans?"

We both stand when we see the doctor coming into the waiting room.

"Hi, I'm Dr. Reynolds." He shakes both of our hands.

"How is he?" I ask.

"The first 48 hours are going to be critical. He sustained some broken ribs and a broken collarbone along with some cuts and bruises. He's very fortunate that he wasn't struck on the driver's side because he may not have survived."

"Can we see him please?" RayVen asks.

"As soon as he's out of recovery we'll give you the room number."

While we wait on that, I call Mama to make sure she and Harland are ok with X. By the time I get off the phone, a nurse is coming to give us Ty's room number. I nod at Carmine and he follows us upstairs. They have him set up in ICU so they can keep a close watch on his injuries. They didn't want to take a chance on him slipping into a coma or no shit like that. The nurse tells us we can only go in two at a time because of some kinda bullshit policy. So I let RayVen go in to have her time with him. With all the wires and tubes they have hooked up to him, I know they gave him something to sleep. They did a good job cleaning him up and everything. And they have a bandage around his head to protect his stitches. I'm glad of that because I didn't want my baby flipping out again. There's also a cast that runs from the top of his shoulder down to his wrist. Even though they have a blanket over him, I can see the bandages wrapped around his stomach. I watch through the glass as RayVen covers her mouth with her hands and begins to cry again. She pulls a chair close to the bed, taking a seat next to him. I hated to see lil' dude laid up like this and even more to see my wife hurting because of it. As I look at RayVen stressing over Ty, I can't help having flashbacks of when she was in the hospital. The whole time she was in there I was sitting beside her bed, watching her sleep. Praying for the chance to see her smile again. If she was strong enough to fight through her situation, then I know lil' homie can do the same.

"They made it down yet?" I ask Carmine.

He nods. "V.J. just went downstairs to meet them. Enzo put a bullet in the two muthafuckas who were supposed to be watching our backs at Harland's crib."

I only nod.

"How you wanna handle this, bro?"

"Tell Tony to come up. I want him to keep eyes on Ray."

He sends a text and a few minutes later we see Tony walking down the hallway. We both nod and give him a pound. There isn't much need for words when there is business to handle. For some reason the IV starts beeping, causing the nurse to get up from her station to check things out. After she changes a few bags it eventually stops making noise. I watch as she places a hand on RayVen's shoulder and says something to her. RayVen nods, causing the nurse to leave out real quick and go down the hall. Soon as the nurse leaves, she motions for me to come to her.

"X I'm going to stay the night to make sure things go okay with Ty," RayVen tells me. "Can you make sure the baby's ok?"

I nod. "I'll hit you up to let you know he's straight. I'ma leave Tony here to keep an eye on you though. Make sure you get home safe and everything."

Both of us look over at Ty and I brush away a tear that was sliding down her cheek.

"He's going to be ok, right?" she asks.

I put my arm around her, holding her close. "Lil' dude is tough. I know he'll pull through just fine."

The nurse comes back a few minutes later with some blankets and pillows for RayVen. For a minute I thought she was gonna trip when I told her Tony is staying with RayVen, but all she did was ask if he needs a blanket. Once the two of them are set up, me and Carmine head downstairs to meet up with the rest of the crew. When we finally make it outside, I see V.J. and Enzo looking at something on a tablet.

"Wassup?" I ask them.

"I guess those punk muthafuckas was good for something before we bodied them," V.J. says. "They gotta picture of the driver of the Chevy."

He hands the tablet to me and I see pictures of Nolo getting out of the Chevy and walking into some kind of building.

"Whose spot is this?" I ask.

"Some kinda chop shop or something. The owner and his crew do work for Marciano."

I nod. "Cool, let's pay them muthafuckas a visit."

They follow me to Harland's crib so I can drop off my car and peek in on X. I'm glad his lil' ass is sleep because he probably would have flipped if he didn't see his mama. Enzo hooks us up with some heat before posting up in the yard to keep an eye on things. As long as our family is covered, my bros and I can handle the rest. It takes us about a good twenty minutes to reach this big ass car dealership on the other side of town. There's a garage on the back of the building where they run the chop shop. If someone didn't know what to look for they would just think it was a regular part of the dealership. The neighborhood is fucked up, and from the feel of it, I know shady shit goes down around here on the regular. So we gotta watch how we move, because the police are always lurking in case some shit go down. From the dim lighting and the few sparks flashing through the window every so often, we knew somebody was in there working.

"So, how y'all wanna roll on these fools?" Carmine asks.

"Well, Mama always told us to knock before going in a room," V.J. says.

I shrug. "Then knock nigga."

V.J. laughs as he revs up the engine of his Hummer and drives that muthafucka straight through the front door. There are about six dudes on the inside who take off running. There's about five cars on the inside being stripped down, but none of them resemble the Chevy Nolo was driving. While Carmine leans out the back window, I lean out the passenger side, and we let our guns do the talking for us. I make sure to hit two of them in the back which leaves a nice hole in their chests. The last one I hit in both his kneecaps. That nigga don't need his legs to tell us what we need to know. After Carmine takes care of the other three, we get out to holla at the dude who is on the floor screaming.

"My legs, my fuckin' legs!!" he screams.

I kick him until he rolls over onto his back. "Where the fuck is Nolo?" I ask.

"Man, I don't know! I ain't seen him since he dropped a car off earlier."

Carmine kicks him in the ribs. "You mean a Chevy, right?"

He nods his head real fast, looking like a bobble head doll. "Yeah that's it. He wanted us to do some work on it."

"Why?"

"It had some red paint on it and was kinda bent up in the front. I guess he ran into somebody or something," he says. "One of Marciano's boys came to get it not too long ago. That's all I know man; please don't kill me."

"Where do we find 'em?" I ask.

"Man fuck! I told you I don't know!"

I nod at Carmine and he grabs a jug of gasoline. He pours it all over the dude and the cars that are nearby. When the jug is empty we walk back towards the Hummer.

"Hey, y'all muthafuckas just gonna leave me here?" dude asks. "Well fuck y'all! I hope Marciano bodies all you muthafuckas."

Once inside the Hummer, I fire off a few shots, causing the bullets to graze the wet concrete. The heat from the impact immediately starts a fire inside the garage. We hear dude screaming when the flames spread and jump on his ass. The tires screech against the pavement when V.J. backs out of the shop and into the street. A few minutes pass and a sound of the building exploding echoes throughout the dark street. It doesn't take long for the wail of sirens to be heard in the distance. While the police and other emergency officials are flying past us to the garage, we creep in the opposite direction, disappearing down the street.

CHAPTER 21

$\mathcal{I}$'ve been back and forth to the hospital so much I'm sure the staff is starting to think I've taken up residency there. But I can't go a day without making sure my son is ok. People have always questioned how I can raise a teenager that's not biologically mine. And my answer to them is, the same way I raise my younger son. Just because Ty spent most of his life in the system doesn't mean he has a disability. Obviously, he needs me in a different way than X, but that doesn't mean I'm going to treat him differently. I've been trying not to get too attached to him because I know the day will come where he may want to leave or try to search for any of his remaining biological family. He's never mentioned it but I would never deny him the chance to learn more about his roots. Every time I see him lying in that hospital bed with his face all bruised, hooked up to all those machines to make his recovery as painless as possible, I can't help thinking about his birth parents that were killed in a car accident. That's why I make it my business to be here for him every day. To pray for him and encourage him to keep fighting.

Of course, the police haven't found any leads yet. The windows of the truck that hit Ty were heavily tinted so no one could lay eyes on the driver. Nor had anyone seen where the truck disappeared to. With no leads or clear evidence, it's safe to say they probably have brushed off furthering their investigation. I just feel so helpless. There's absolutely nothing I can do to bring Ty home right now. I miss him sneaking into the house at all hours of the night. And his little devilish smirk when he's up to something. A tear slides down the curve of my cheek as I think about how proud he was when he showed me his college acceptance letter.

"Mommy don't cry," X tells me. He uses his pudgy little fingers to wipe away my tears.

He and I are sitting in the picnic area at the center eating lunch.

With everything that's been going on with our family, I knew I was going to drive myself crazy if I continued to sit at home all day. Besides, it isn't fair to X to keep him cooped up in the house for so long. So this morning I got myself up and headed to work. It would have been too hectic for me to jump back in with a full caseload. My mind is nowhere near in a place where I can be useful to anyone. But I have taken time to check in with everyone to make sure they have what they need. That is, when I'm not tied up with all this mandatory paperwork. I'm just grateful for Tanya and my other coworkers who have pitched in to help me the way they have.

"Why you sad, Mommy?" X asks me while he rubs my cheek.

"Just worried about Ty sweetie, that's all."

He nods. "Me too. We go to see him?"

I smile a little bit. "Yeah, I'll take you to see him later."

"Good, I make him a picture to feel better."

No matter how I'm feeling, my baby can always bring a smile to my face. "I think he'll like that, sweet pea."

X hugs me then. "Mommy...you mad at Daddy?"

I know X is smart for his age, but I didn't expect *that* question to come out his mouth. "What makes you say that?"

"We left home to live with Pop Pop."

I nod. "Mommy and Daddy just had a fight. We went to Pop Pop's house so I can think a little bit."

"When we go home? I miss being with Daddy."

Even though he's too young to understand, I don't want to lie to my son. Truth be told, I honestly don't know when we'll be going home. Things between Xavien and I are still in a rocky place. But I do appreciate him being there to comfort me when everything happened with Ty. He's even texted me a few times to let me know he's gone by to check on him.

"Come on, it's time to go back inside."

"Okay," X says and follows me back to daycare.

Once he's situated, I take a slow walk back to the main building in hopes of spending the next few hours quietly in my office. But from the way this crowd is set up in the lobby that might not be happening. It seems like every staff member had stopped working to be there. Many of the kids are here also.

What in the hell is going on here? I think as I approach the group. When I get a little closer I see Marciano Barajas, of all people, in the center of the crowd. I hadn't seen him since that day I kicked him out of my office. He's giving a speech like he was just elected Mayor or something.

"I thank all of you for your vote of confidence," Marciano says. "If we work together I guarantee we can take Epic Changes nationally. My mission is to create a place of healing not only for the children of Atlanta, but for every child across this great country."

Everyone within the sound of his voice starts to clap. Since Tanya is the nearest to me, I tap her on the shoulder.

"Hey girl, what's going on?" I ask her.

"From the looks of things, Tim got Marciano to invest in Epic," she tells me. "Can you believe it?"

A sick feeling settles in the pit of my stomach. "You have got to be kidding me."

"Nope, while you were out with your baby he presented Tim with a check in front of everyone to make it official."

I shake my head still not believing what I'm hearing. My supervisor, Tim Mitchell, has just sold his soul and the future of this company for a few measly dollars. And it seems like no one can see how bad of an idea this is except me. I glance over at Marciano who is grinning from ear to ear as he shakes everyone's hand. When he looks through the crowd at me I swear I see horns growing out of his head. He takes a break from the adulation and walks over to where I'm standing.

"It's a pleasure to see you again, RayVen," he says still grinning. "It looks as if we're going to be business partners after all."

"Looks can be deceiving," I tell him.

"With your husband agreeing to do some work for me, I'm sure you would've been on board."

"What are you talking about?"

A smile spreads across his face. "I'll let him tell you. Maybe we can have lunch one day in the future to discuss things."

I shake my head in disgust and make my way towards the front door.

This shit doesn't make any sense. Why would Xavien agree to do business with someone like Marciano, knowing how I felt about him? Something about this whole scenario didn't feel right. I have to go outside to get some air before this bullshit suffocates me. As if my day can't get any worse, I see Marianna sitting at the desk. I haven't seen that bitch since before those pictures were delivered to my house. And I damn sure am not in the mood to see her now.

She gets that infamous smirk on her face. "While you're out, let that sexy ass husband of yours know I enjoyed every bit of him last week. I see he hasn't lost his touch."

Now I done told this bitch not to fuck with me. All I was trying to do is go outside to cool off so I can keep a level head. But to hell with that shit. Before any more slick shit can come out of her mouth, I run over and grab a handful of her hair, snatching her skinny ass across the desk. The impact she makes with the floor is enough to grab everyone's attention.

"Oh shit! Ms. RayVen going ham y'all!" one of the kids screams out.

I am on top of her, and my left hand still has a tight grip on her hair while my right connects with her face repeatedly. Marianna starts screaming and digging her nails in my arm, which only makes me hit her harder.

"TALK THAT SHIT NOW BITCH!" Wham! "HUH, I DON'T HEAR YOU BITCH?!" Wham! "I TOLD YOU…!" Wham! "NOT TO…!" Wham! "FUCK…!" Wham! "WITH ME!" Wham! Wham! Wham!

From the commotion around us, I know everyone in the center had gathered into the lobby.

"Get her, Ms. RayVen!" the kids cheer in excitement.

I guess it's kind of wild for them to see this side of me. Nobody knew this side of me existed. And to be perfectly honest, I never knew I had this much pent-up rage in me until she pushed my buttons. A small part of me feels bad because I'm usually the one who's a big advocate against fighting. Whether at home or here at the center, my main goal has always been to work things out peacefully. But at this very moment, I couldn't give two fucks about any of that shit. This ass whooping I'm putting on Marianna is long overdue.

"Oh my god, RayVen calm down!" I hear someone say as they try to pull me off her.

Without looking back, I shove whoever it is away from me and continue to hit Marianna. The blood I see dripping from her nose is like pouring gasoline on the fire of my rage. I gave the bitch a pass when she laid eyes on my husband. He's fine; I can't stop a bitch from looking at him. But she fucked up when she put her hands on him.

Then she had the muthafuckin' gall to think she could get away with rubbing that shit in my face. No, I'm ending this bitch right here and now. Several pairs of hands grab me from behind, finally pulling me off her. Since they want to hold my arms I kick her several times.

"YOU'RE GONNA PAY FOR PUTTING YOUR HANDS ON ME YOU FAT BITCH!" she screams. One of her eyes is starting to swell and there's blood dripping from her face.

I run towards her, ready to put my foot in her ass again, but they pull me backwards down the hallway.

"Get the fuck off me." I wrestle my way out of their grip and walk to my office, slamming the door behind me.

I drop down in the chair behind the desk and sit there for I don't know how long. When I begin to calm down, I notice that my right leg is shaking and tears are streaming down my face. But I know they are from anger and frustration more than anything else. I can't lie; it felt damn good to finally lay hands on that bitch. The muscles in my arm are sore from hitting her so much. The sound of footsteps approaching my door causes me to dry my face. I'd shown my ass enough for today. The last thing I want is for anyone to see me crying. The door swings open and Mr. Mitchell comes storming into my office.

"Would you mind telling me what the hell just happened out there?" he says to me. "One of the most prominent members of this city comes to give his support to the center, and you attack a fellow coworker right in front of him. Not only have you embarrassed this facility, but you've embarrassed yourself. I expected better from you, RayVen."

No, this muthafucka didn't. If he keeps trying me Marianna won't be the only one catching these hands today. I stand up to look him in the eye. He must have seen something in them because he takes a few steps back like he felt threatened. Punk ass. "You expected better of me? Is that what you just said?" I ask. "True, I put an ass whooping on that bitch, but she had it coming. If you weren't so busy shoving your dick in her throat you would've noticed that she's caused nothing but trouble since she walked through those doors. So, I'm not embarrassed about a damn thing, Tim."

He looks shocked for a minute that I called him out on fucking Marianna. "At any rate RayVen, Mr. Barajas stopped Marianna from pressing charges against you; however, I am obligated to suspend you indefinitely."

"Are you fucking serious right now? After everything I've invested into this company? After everything I've invested into these kids? Tim, the majority of the older kids are doing well and most may actually graduate on time because of the time and energy *I* put into them. And just because some rich asshole flashed a few dollars in your face, you shit on one of the few people who actually gives a damn about these kids?!"

His punk ass drops his eyes, unable to look at me. "I'm really sorry about this RayVen. I don't know what else to say."

I shake my head at him. "Believe it or not you've said more than enough."

I grab my purse and walk to the daycare to get my son. While walking to my car I hear someone calling my name. I turn in the direction of the voice to see Tanya running towards me.

"Hey, I was just coming to see if you're ok," she says.

I shrug. "I'm fine."

"Girl, I did not know you had hands like that!" Tanya was grinning from ear to ear. "When I saw you snatch that bitch across the counter I was like, YESSSS Bitch!!"

I laugh a little.

"So, I guess Tim is sending you home on probation to save face, right?"

I shake my head. "No, his punk ass put me under "indefinite suspension' or in layman's terms, I'm fired."

"Are you fucking serious? RayVen you've been the backbone of this place since the day you started here. Nobody has been able to get through to these kids like you have. And he plays you just like that?"

I shake my head in an attempt to keep myself from crying. But with X in my arms, there is no way I can stop my tears from falling.

"I'm so sorry, RayVen." Tanya wraps an arm around my shoulders to console me.

"Yo, Ms. RayVen."

I look up to see a few of the kids coming out of the building towards me.

"Mr. Mitchell told us you're not working here anymore. That ain't true, is it?" one of them asks.

I nod. "I owe all of you an apology. I should have handled that situation better. Maybe if I had, I'd still have my job."

"Nah, it was cool to see you throw hands Ms. RayVen," another one tells me. "You can't let a bitch play you any kinda way."

I laugh a little.

"What we gonna do without you? You know half the people here don't give a shit about us."

I sigh heavily. "I want all of you to continue to work hard so you can graduate and become successful. Like I told each and every one of you, your dreams are possible. All you have to do is reach for them."

They only nod.

"When things get straightened out I promise me and X will come back to see you. But if you need me before then, you have my number. Even though I won't be here you can always reach out to me."

They all come and wrap their arms around me to say their goodbyes. A few of them break down crying, and it takes everything in me not to cry with them. Besides, I don't want X to see me crying anymore. Reluctantly, I give everybody one last hug. One of them holds X for me while I get the door open and the bags inside. He waves goodbye to them as I strap him securely in the car seat.

"Bye Ms. RayVen. Bye lil' X.... we gonna miss y'all!" they call after us, as I crank up the car and drive home.

CHAPTER 22

Xavien

"**O**H MY GOD!! PULL ME UP! PLEASE!!" dude screams. He glances down at the city below us and starts crying. Not that I blame his ass though. I'm holding him by his ankles as I hang him over the balcony. We had to be over twenty stories up.

"PULL ME UP PLEASE!!" he begs.

"SHUT THE FUCK UP MUTHAFUCKA!!"

The people in the room behind us are yelling and screaming while my brothers keep them from interfering. I glance over at the podium where Marciano is standing. There is no denying he is pissed off that his squeaky-clean image is about to be fucked up.

Since Marciano felt the need to pop up at my job when he wanted to get his point across, then I thought it was only fair that I do the same. It's been all over the news how he was being honored at some big event for being Entrepreneur of the Year, or some shit like that. You know the type of shit where there are a bunch of rich muthafuckas bragging about how much money they got. Champagne, fake smiles and a bunch of publicity. That muthafucka thought he had me on a leash 'cause I agreed to put some work in for him, but at the end of the day I was fronting just like he was. He ain't had to do my lil' homie Ty like that. But he was about to find out that my clap game is a lot stronger than his. Let's see if all these rich muthafuckas will continue to fuck with him when they find out how he really rolls.

The event is being held at the Four Seasons at their ballroom, which is set up on the penthouse floor. We couldn't pull up on these uppity muthafuckas any kinda way, so we had to shift gears a little bit. When we came through earlier to reserve a room, riding in a stretch limo and dressed in Armani suits, we were able to slide on through without the staff looking at us sideways. Everything was either yes sir, no sir, or is there anything else we can do for you? In places like these, the deeper your pockets run, the less they fuck with you. While taking the next few hours to scope everything out, we noticed that the security team was bullshit. If they were legit, they might have found the guns, ski masks, and gloves in our suitcases. But then we'd have to start dropping bodies. Which wasn't a part of the plan. Besides, we didn't want to draw unnecessary attention to ourselves.

Since that bullshit event didn't start for another thirty minutes, I hit RayVen up to see how they are doing.

Hey baby, just checking in on y'all.

My phone buzzes a few seconds later. *X is fine. He misses you.*

From the way she's texting, I know something has her pissed off. *Ray, what's going on with you?*

TTYL X.

See, I hate when she does that shit. Gonna have me worried about her ass all night. Apple ass head.

I shake my head and put my phone back in my pocket.

"Yo, you good X?" V.J. asked.

"Yeah, you know how my wife is."

Carmine started laughing. "Last time y'all had an argument this bad, Ray ended up pregnant with X," he said. "She might be having twins when y'all make up from this shit."

"For real though," V.J. laughs.

"Man, y'all muthafuckas ain't shit." I could only shake my head at them.

I couldn't even be mad at my bros for clowning me because they weren't lying. After we fell out about her leaving Jersey, it was over three months when I laid eyes on her again. New Year's Eve was that weekend, so I asked Harland to help me surprise her. When I saw her standing there with that black dress on, rocking a short haircut, looking sexy as fuck, I knew there was no way I was leaving there without her. But after apologizing for treating her the way I did, she showed me that she still had mad love for me. And by the time we finished making up, I had no doubt that I'd gotten her pregnant. A month later, I noticed her sneaking out of bed every night to use the bathroom down the hall. One time I followed her and heard her throwing up. I asked her about it the next day but she just brushed the shit off. I'd learned enough about her to know she don't ever throw up when she's sick. But I let her slide for another month or so before taking her ass to the doctor. Come to find out, her ass was ten weeks deep in her pregnancy.

"Anyway…" I slammed the mag into my gun making sure it's locked in place before switching off the safety. "Y'all muthafuckas ready or nah."

There's a private elevator that leads up to the penthouse area. On the way up, we throw on some gloves and a mask. With all the high-profile muthafuckas inside the room, you would've thought there would have been at least ten dudes guarding the door instead of five. We'd knocked two of them out already by the time the other dudes knew what was going down. Me and V.J. dragged them to a nearby supply closet while Carmine kept watch. Once phase one was handled, it was time to see about our homie Marciano.

As we walked down the hall, we could hear the speaker going on and on about Marciano's greatest accomplishments in the city.

"Not to take anything away from any of you great business owners, but our next award recipient is known for his many acts of selflessness and generosity," the speaker said. "Many of our small businesses have been given the opportunity to flourish to become everything they are today because of him. It's my honor and extreme pleasure to present the Entrepreneur of the Year award to Marciano Barajas."

Everyone in the room got on their feet to give him a standing ovation. We watched as he made his way through the crowd to the podium.

"Please, ladies and gentlemen have a seat," Marciano told them. "I'm just a hardworking citizen of this community trying to give back to my friends and neighbors…"

The crowd starts clapping again.

"If we don't kick this door in soon, I'm gonna shoot myself in the head from hearing so much bullshit," Carmine says.

"But I'm extremely honored to accept the Entrepreneur of the Year award. I just wish that there were more of these so I can have all of you onstage with me. If it wasn't for your unending support in my vision, none of this would have ever been possible."

"Enough of this fake ass bullshit. Kick this muthafucka in," I tell them.

Boom!! The door shatters off the hinges when my bros dig their heels into that muthafucka. We fire off a few rounds into the ceiling, causing everyone to jump up and start screaming.

"EVERYBODY SHUT THE FUCK UP!!!"

"What is the meaning of this?" Marciano asks, trying to grow some balls. He's still standing at the podium.

I fire off a shot in his direction, barely missing his ass. "Don't act like you don't know what this is, homie."

Carmine takes a brown manila envelope from underneath his coat. "Who's the muthafucka in charge?"

Some skinny dude with glasses steps forward.

"There's something in this envelope you need to see." Carmine tosses it at his feet.

He kicks the envelope in response. "I don't need anything from thugs like you."

"Did this muthafucka say we was thugs?" V.J. asks.

"I think he did bro," Carmine says.

"Well, let's show this muthafucka how raw we can get."

I toss V.J. my gun and snatch dude up by the collar of his shirt.

"UNHAND ME!" He struggles, but he's unable to get out of my grip.

I carry him over to the glass doors that lead out to the balcony, kicking them open with one foot.

"OH GOD! WHAT ARE YOU DOING?" he screams when I hang him over the railing of the balcony. "OH GOD! PLEASE, PLEASE PULL ME UP!! I DON'T WANT TO DIE!!"

"All this shit could have been avoided if you would've just looked at what was in the envelope," Carmine tells him.

"PLEASE LET ME GO!!"

"Aight." I let go of one his legs and everyone in the room starts screaming.

"GOD! HELP ME!!" dude starts crying again.

"You gonna look in the envelope now?"

"I'll do whatever you want, just pull me back."

I look over at Carmine and he gives me a nod. Eventually, I snatch dude back to the other side of the balcony. He breaks down crying when he feels the floor underneath him.

"Thank God," he says.

"Don't blame God for what went down tonight. Thank your Entrepreneur of the Year, Marciano Barajas," Carmine tells them. "You see he slipped out of here while everything was happening."

The crowd turns around to see that he was gone.

"Where is he?" I hear someone ask.

"Oh my god! Look at these pictures Jeffrey." A lady runs to the balcony with the envelope we tried to give dude earlier.

My bros were able to get some receipts on that muthafucka dirty dealing. There are also copies of all the checks made out to him from the business owners Marciano is hustling.

"I don't understand any of this," the dude named Jeffrey says. "Why would Marciano do these things?"

"'Cause he's a crooked muthafucka, that's why," I tell him.

"Looks like you're associated with thugs after all, Jeffrey," Carmine tells him.

While everyone is caught up trying to see the pictures, we roll out to the elevators. Once on the main floor, we head out one of the side exits. There's an alley a block away from the hotel where V.J.'s Hummer is parked. We were just about to cross the street when my phone goes off. I look at the screen to see an unlisted number.

I swipe the answer button. "Who dis?"

"Heard you been looking for me, nigga." I immediately recognize Nolo's voice. "I guess you got in your feelings when I popped your lil' homie. Muthafucka shoulda zigged instead of zagged."

"I ain't one for this back and forth shit muthafucka. When you ready to square up get at me." I end the call. *Pussy ass nigga.*

Carmine and V.J. are on the other side waiting for me. I put my phone back in my pocket so I can catch up with them. As I'm crossing the street, I hear some tires burning up the pavement. Soon as I look up I see that black Chevy speeding towards me. I snatch my gun out the back of my pants and fire off a few rounds through the windshield. The glass cracks causing him to swerve, barely missing me. Instead of stopping he continues to speed down the street. I was too busy still trying to shoot that muthafucka to notice my bros were already in the Hummer and had pulled up next to me.

"X, let's roll!"

When I got my senses back, I could hear the distant sound of sirens approaching. I'd forgotten all about the shit we pulled upstairs a few minutes earlier. I hop in the back and we peel off down the road. That muthafucka had slipped by us tonight. But I'ma make sure the next time we meet up will be his last night breathing.

CHAPTER 23

RayVen

I've been trying not to be in my feelings too hard about losing my job. It's not like I'm pressed for money or anything. Plus, more time off will mean I can spend more time with X. But I'm just so used to working, and I definitely miss the kids at the center. My phone has been blowing up with texts messages from them needing advice. Or just needing to vent. So much so that I invited them all to lunch this afternoon. There's a restaurant that's walking distance from the center that serves the best pizza and hamburgers. I was planning on treating them out before everything took a negative turn anyway. All of them have been doing so well in school, and I just wanted them to know how proud I am of them. And I see no reason to go back on my word.

"Ms. RayVen, the center ain't been the same without you," says Cameron, a fifteen-year-old runaway. Her stepmother tried to trade her for drugs the night she left home.

I smile. "I miss you guys too. How have things been going?"

"The same bullshit as always," Omari tells me. He just turned sixteen and recently gave up the street life to go back to school.

"What's going on?"

"Mitchell been on a power trip since that dude Marciano came by. Him and the lady at the desk be in the office a lot after hours."

"Yeah, I peeped that shit too. I think they smashing," another one of the kids chimes in. "But she ain't had as much attitude lately since Ms. RayVen put them paws to her."

All of them crack up laughing then.

"Pizza!" X yells when the waitress brings two large pizzas with extra breadsticks.

"X, what kinda pizza you want, all meat or pepperoni?" Omari asks him.

"Ummm…" He puts his fingers to his chin like he's seriously thinking it over. I laugh and shake my head. I am too through with this little boy. "Meat."

"Aight, I got you." Omari puts a small slice on his plate.

The rest of our lunch goes by smoothly. The kids get more than a belly full, plus they were able to talk to me about everything that has been bothering them. I'd started having group therapy with them a while back so they can learn how to share their struggles and lean on each other for support. Before we say our goodbyes, I order them two more pizzas to take with them for dinner.

"Aight, see you next time, Ms. RayVen." I give each one a hug and watch them until they make it safely back on the center's parking lot.

I was strapping X into his car seat when my cell starts to ring. After making sure he's secure, only then do I answer it.

"Hello," I say into my Bluetooth.

"Hi, is this Mrs. Verano?"

"It is."

"Good afternoon, Mrs. Verano. This is Nurse Jennings from the hospital. I am calling you with an update on TySean Evans."

"Is everything ok?" My heart drops because I feared the worse.

"Hold on for a second..." she tells me.

I hear a sound like someone clearing their throat. "Hey Ma..." His voice is a little raspy but there is no mistaking Ty's voice.

I break down crying right there in the parking lot. "Oh my god, it's so good to hear your voice. I'm on my way to see you okay."

"Okay Ma."

I double check the seatbelt in X's seat before hopping in the car and rushing to the hospital. Thank God the traffic isn't too terrible. I think I make it there in record time. With X in one arm and my purse in the other, I damn near run to the elevators. After what feels like an eternity, I am walking down the hall to Ty's room. Tears begin to fall from my eyes when I see him sitting up in bed watching TV. The bandages have been removed from around his head, revealing his stitches. And a sling had now replaced the cast that was on his arm. He smiles as soon as he sees us.

"Ty!!!" X screams. He jumps out of my arms and runs to climb in bed with him.

"How you doing lil' bruh," Ty asks as he hugs X with his good arm.

"I missed you."

"Missed you too lil' homie." He looks over at me. "Ma, I'm aight. Stop crying."

"I'm sorry." I grab some Kleenex to dry my face.

"Come sit Mommy," X tells me.

I pull up a nearby chair after giving him a hug and a kiss on the cheek. "I've been praying night and day for you to pull through this."

He nods. "I know; it might sound crazy but I could hear your voice. Even though I wasn't able to talk to you. It was like I was sleeping but awake at the same time."

I can only nod.

"I heard when X came by too. He kept telling me to fight through it and y'all were going to always have my back." He shakes his head a little. "But this shit is my fault though. I shoulda said something sooner."

"Sweetheart, you did nothing wrong."

"Ma, X ain't cheat on you," he tells me.

I shake my head. "Ty, you don't have to..."

"Nah, Ma listen. I was gonna spend the night at grandpa crib that night so I can holla at you one-on-one." He takes a deep breath. "I will understand if you wanna get rid of me after this, but I rather keep it a hunnid."

"Ty, what do you have to tell me?"

He sighs again. "I was fuckin' Marianna. I met her at a bar one night and we started smashing. Then she started asking me about X and I cut her ass off. When those pictures showed up at the house of her and X, I went back to the bar that night and confronted her about it. She admitted to setting X up. Then me and the dude she was sitting with got into it. And he said he was gonna take me out."

A stray tear slides down his cheek and I see him swallow back more. "Ma, I'm sorry. I ain't mean to get y'all caught up in no bullshit. If you hate me right now I deserve that shit...but I'm sorry." He lost his battle with tears because they begin to flow freely down his cheeks.

I sit on the bed next to him and wrap my arms around him as much as I can without hurting him.

"I'm so sorry, Ma," Ty says again.

"Shhh...it's okay, sweetheart." I cradle him close to me. "It's okay. You did nothing wrong. None of this is your fault."

"I been feeling guilty about it ever since. Y'all was cool before this shit started happening."

"This runs a lot deeper than you sleeping with the wrong woman." I cover X's ears for a second. "Did you use protection?"

"Yeah, Ma. Always."

I sigh in relief. "Thank God because she was also messing around with my boss," I tell him.

"For real?"

I nod. "Yeah, she said some slick shit about Xavien and I ended up beating her ass."

"Ma, you been throwing hands at the job?!" He bursts out laughing but suddenly grabs his ribs. "Ah shit, I forgot my ribs was still fucked up."

"You need me to call the nurse?" I ask concerned.

"Nah, I'll be aight. It just hurts when I laugh."

I pat him on the leg. "Okay, if you need something for pain don't hesitate to call."

He nods. Ty leans over and grabs the picture X drew him from the table. "Yo, X I'm feeling this new picture lil' bruh. You did this by yourself?"

X starts smiling from ear to ear. "Uh huh."

"When I get home I'm gonna put it up in my room so I can see it all the time. I might even take it to college with me. What you think?"

"Yeah! Please."

Ty laughs, "I got you lil' homie." He holds out his fist for X to bump it.

I laugh at X trying to be grown. But it really warms my heart to see the way they interact. I'm just glad Ty is going to be okay. Praise God for healing and watching over him. We stay with him until visiting hours are almost over. Luckily, the doctor comes by to see him before we leave. If Ty continues to do well, then he will be coming home in a few days.

"Alright mister, you get some rest and don't give these nurses a hard time," I tell him.

He gets that little grin on his face. "Nah, I actually like a woman giving me a bath. Makes me feel like the dude off *Coming to America*."

"Boy, if you don't sit down somewhere." I laugh. "I'll check on you soon as I can tomorrow."

"Aight. But Ma, real talk…"

I turn around to face him. "What?"

"You need to holla at X so y'all can fix things."

I nod. "I will."

X had fallen asleep on the way to the parking lot so the only thing keeping me company are my restless thoughts. Ty had blown my mind when he confessed to sleeping with Marianna. And the fact that she used him to try to get information about Xavien makes me wish I'd finished what I started at the center. I hate to admit it, but Ty was right about Xavien and I needing to have a conversation. Things had gotten out of hand. Probably because I was being so stubborn to begin with. He has tried reaching out to me but all I've ever done is keep him at arm's length. At the end of the day he is my husband. And I do miss him.

I click the unlock button on my keychain and open the door to get X situated. He slept through me locking him in the seat and checking it, which is always a good thing. I put my purse beside him and click the child lock on his door. As soon as I my hand touches the handle I feel a pair of arms tightly grab my waist.

"Wassup, boo. Did you miss me?" he says.

I elbow him hard in the face, causing him to grab the side of his head. *Shit, I left my gun in my purse.*

I snatch open the driver door and climb inside, trying to reach my purse. But he grabs me, throwing me backwards onto the concrete.

He leans forward trying to grab me but I use a submission move I learned from Carmine. I lock one leg around the back of his head and put the other against his throat, choking him. He hits me several times in the side but I continue to choke him until I feel something sharp cut my leg. Immediately, I let him go and grab my thigh, which is bleeding.

"I should just end you right now bitch!" he tells me.

Suddenly, I hear a gun firing. I look up to see him holding his shoulder as he runs in the opposite direction.

"RayVen, you good?" Tony asks me. "My bad, I just went to change clothes."

"I'm ok," I reassure him. "Get X for me please."

I try to stand as he puts X in the back of his truck before grabbing my purse and keys. When everything is situated, he picks me up and carries me to the passenger side.

"You wanna go to your dad's?" he asks me.

I shake my head. "No, I need to see Xavien."

He nods and drives out of the parking lot.

CHAPTER 24

Xavien

I'm pacing back and forth in my driveway as I wait for Tony to pull up. He'd hit me up a few minutes earlier to tell me he was bringing RayVen and X over. On one hand I'm glad to have my family home, but to know that muthafucka came at my wife the way he did… I swear I was fuckin' heated. Marciano finally decided to hit me up after we crashed his little party. I saw on the news how his ass is under investigation. Now that everyone knows how grimy he is, he wanna call me bitchin' and shit.

"Chains, I thought we had a deal," he said. "Do you realize you have single-handedly ruined my reputation?"

"I can't take credit for that cuz I did have a little help. But that deal of ours went out the window when your boy tried to take out my family."

"Well enough is enough; if you and him want at each other then I'll make it happen."

"Where and when?"

"There's an abandoned warehouse that I own on the outskirts of the city. I'll send you the address and the time when he's ready to meet."

"Cool." I hung up then. *Punk ass nigga.*

After about five more minutes of pacing, I see the headlights of Tony's truck turning into my driveway. While he jumps out to grab X from the back seat, I run to the other side to get RayVen. I damn near lose my shit when I see her leg is bleeding. She wraps her arms around my neck and I carry her into the house. Carmine and V.J. jump up as soon as they see us come in.

"Any of y'all gotta first aid kit?"

"Yeah, I got one." V.J. runs down the hall to get it.

"Baby, how you holding up?"

"I'm ok," she says softly.

I rip the rest of her pants leg so I can see how bad she was cut. It's deep enough to leave a scar, but not to the point where she will need stitches. When V.J. brings his first aid kit, I start cleaning her leg.

"Y'all need anything else?" Carmine asks.

I glance over at X, who is still knocked out. I swear his lil' ass can sleep through anything.

"Nah, I got it from here," I tell them.

They nod and leave out the front door.

I can feel RayVen's eyes on me as I continue to clean her leg with gauze and peroxide. So much shit had gone on to the point where neither one of us knew where to start.

"Ty, called me today," she says finally.

Hearing that brings a smile to my face. "That's wassup. I knew his lil' ass would pull through."

"Yeah, soon as I got that phone call I rushed to see him. He asked about you."

I nod as I put a bandage over her wound.

"Thank you," RayVen tells me.

I shake my head. "Why you always thanking me for doing what I'm supposed to do?"

She only shrugs.

"I'ma put X in the bed and I'll come back and help you out."

"Okay."

I unhook him from the seat and carry him up to his room. In the middle of changing his clothes, he wakes up. A big smile spreads across his face when he sees me.

"Hey Daddy," he says with a yawn.

"'Sup dude. You aight?"

He nods. "Gotta potty."

I take him to the bathroom and clean him up a little bit. By the time I'm finished putting on his pajamas, he is knocked out again. I leave his room in time to see RayVen limping up the stairs. We lock eyes for a long time until she starts walking towards our room. Out of habit, I run downstairs to make sure everything is locked up. After taking a quick look through the window, I see Tony is still posted up in the yard. I switch off the lights and go back upstairs to find RayVen sitting on the edge of the bed. She still has her ripped up pants on and everything. My hand begins to rub her back when I take a seat next to her. I'm glad she doesn't push me away.

"X...what's going on with us?" she asks finally.

I sigh heavily. "I honestly don't know where to begin; shit is so crazy."

RayVen looks at me then. "Just start from the beginning."

I shake my head. "All of this started 'cause of this beef Nolo has with me. He ain't never got over the ass whooping I put on him. So he got his fam to help try to take me out."

"Family?" She takes a minute to think and then her eyes get real wide. "You don't mean..."

I nod. "Marciano and Marianna are Nolo's family. When she got the job working with you, she was able to get our information to send it to him. The flowers, the phone calls, the pictures, all that bullshit was set up by them."

RayVen shakes her head. "X, they hurt Ty, they came after me and my baby, they had you and me questioning each other..."

"I know baby...but you was right when you said all this shit is my fault. I shoulda deaded this shit a long time ago."

"Xavien no...don't say that. You didn't know things were going to escalate this far. You were just protecting me that night. We'll get through this together like we do any other time."

I shake my head. "Nah, I got us into this and I'm gonna get us out of this shit. I can't live looking over my shoulder, baby. Even if it means my last breath, I'm gonna make sure you and X are straight."

"Don't say that!" She covers her face with her hands. "X…I can't lose you."

I kneel down in front of her so we are eye-to-eye. "Ray, look at me…" I take her hand in mine. "The last thing I wanna do is leave y'all. But these muthafuckas ain't gonna stop coming at us until I square off with them. If my life ends because of it, I'm gonna make sure I take them muthafuckas with me. At least I'll rest knowing you and my son are safe, you feel me."

She wraps her arms around me and starts crying. "Xavien…I'm so sorry…I was so mad at you because I thought…"

I hold her until she finally calms down. Using my fingers, I brush the tears from her face.

"Leave it in the past baby," I tell her. "What matters now is squashing the bullshit between us. I'ma get the shower ready for you, aight."

She nods.

Since she likes the water steaming hot, I make sure I turn the nozzle all the way up. The water may have been running five minutes before I hear her soft footsteps come into the bathroom. She had already undressed, allowing my eyes to roam freely over that sexy ass body. I slide the door of the shower back for her but she walks straight to me, pressing her body into mine. Her big brown eyes looking up at me saying everything that her mouth won't allow her to say. She lifts up my shirt and I snatch that shit off, tossing it on the floor. Her hands roam all over my chest before she starts stroking my neck with her fingers. While standing on her toes, she wraps both arms around my neck to kiss me. And I gladly cover her mouth with mine. She moans when my tongue slides deep, opening up her throat. Somehow, I'm able to slide off my shorts before lifting her up and carrying her in the shower.

The hot ass water ain't had shit on the heat that was burning between us. Because of all the bullshit that had popped off, I ain't fucked my wife in over a month. And from the way this shit is looking, it might be the last time. So I'ma make this shit count tonight. I grab a handful of her thick ass hips and carry her over to the nearest wall. RayVen must have been in the same frame of mind as I was, because she wasn't tripping about that cut on her leg. She just wrapped both of them muthafuckas around my waist.

"Make love to me, X..." she whispers in my ear.

"I ain't gonna be able to hold back on you tonight," I warn her. Usually, she'll beg me to put all my dick in her, but I end up pulling back because she can't take it. But she ain't had much of a choice tonight. I kiss her neck as I slowly guide my dick deep inside my wife. That pussy is so fuckin' tight, squeezing my shit as I navigate my way to the sweetest part of her walls. I never had to doubt whether or not this pussy was mine.

"Xavien!! OH GOD...OH MY GOD!!" RayVen screams when I start long stroking that shit.

This reminds me of that night when I finally got her alone in my crib. She'd been teasing me with that juicy ass pussy for months. And to finally have her ass where I wanted her...I fucked the shit out of her that night. Just like I'm doing right now. I have her pinned against the wall so there's no chance of her moving. The pain from her nails digging into my back couldn't overshadow how amazing her pussy feels. I don't give a fuck how bad she scratches my shit up, just as long as she keeps taking this dick.

"OH MY GOODDD!...X, MY STOMACH...PLEASE X...MY STOMACH."

I shift my hips a little to find that spot but I ain't pulling shit out. I'm hitting that muthafucka stronger than I ever have. No matter what her mouth was saying, I can feel them walls gripping me.

"OOOH GOD!!!...OH GOOODDDD!!!!..."

I ain't gonna lie, I nutted with her. But I ain't nowhere near done with her ass. I kiss her again and we finally get around to washing. After we dry off and everything, I take her in my arms again, carrying her to our king-sized bed. Once she's in the middle, I take a minute to admire the sexiness of her body before exploring her with my mouth. I start at her forehead, then kiss the tip of her nose. When I get to her sexy ass lips, I take my time to enjoy how soft and sweet they are. She moans softly when my lips graze her ears.

"Eres tan jodidamente hermosa," I whisper in her ear. I needed her to know how sexy she is.

"Xavien..." she moans.

From the way she said my name I know she's wet. Every time I speak Spanish to her that pussy starts leaking.

"Quieres que pare?"

She shakes her head. "Please don't stop."

I rub my nose in her neck, inhaling the sweet scent of her body. RayVen gasps loudly when I run my thick ass tongue across her neck. Using the tip, I draw a trail all the way down to the center of her titties. I lick around the entire surface of the left one while kneading the pliable flesh in my hands. Then I work my way to the right, showing it the same attention. She's moaning and squirming under my grip but I'm a man on a mission. And I ain't letting up no time soon. Once her nipples were nice and tight, I begin to work on them muthafuckas like I'm dying of thirst, and the only way to get nourishment is through them. I push them together so I can have access to both at the same time. Moving my head back and forth, I allow my tongue to taste each one before sucking on them like a newborn.

"Oooh…. Ssss….Oooh." RayVen's hands lace through my hair urging me on.

"Te gusta la lengua de papa?"

She nods again and I gently bite her nipple, causing her to squeal.

"Dime que te gusta."

"I love Daddy's tongue."

"Good girl," I tell her before traveling further down.

I kiss her stomach, stopping only to dip my tongue in her navel. There wasn't a spot on her body that I didn't kiss, but I'd intentionally saved the best for last. By now she's climaxed at least three times. I stop to stare at her, breathing hard, body trembling with anticipation because she doesn't know what I'm about to do next. True, I could've ended her suffering a long time ago. Regardless of what happens after tonight, she needs to know that nobody's tongue game can touch mine.

And she's damn sure gonna remember nobody will ever fuck her as good as I do. She can be halfway across the room and all I gotta do is look at her to take her there. Just because I ain't a savage in the streets don't mean I won't be a savage in the sheets. I suck on her calves as I guide her legs to my shoulders. My hands caress those soft ass thighs while they grip her hips firmly, allowing my lips to meet the softness of her plush pussy. The sweet smell of her makes my mouth water. Sticking out my tongue, I taste her gently causing her to cry.

"Shhh…" I rub her hips gently. "Stop crying, baby. Abre y deja que te pruebe."

I pull her closer as I imagine my tongue being the key unlocking the door to her pussy. Her thighs quiver as I gain access to what rightfully belongs to me. Even though the thickness of her legs is covering my ears, I can tell she has a pillow to her mouth to suppress her screams. My mouth works its way up her body again until my body covers hers. I snatch that damn pillow out her hand. She knew better than to hold back with me.

"Estas listo para mi?"

She answers my question by spreading her legs for me.

I wrap an arm around the back of her neck and the other around her leg, making sure she can't run. RayVen sounds like she's fighting for air when the head slips inside her. My hand grips the pillow underneath her head as I lose myself in her body. I had beat it up in the shower so I am gonna keep my promise to make love to her.

"Xavien…" she whispers, placing a hand on my shoulder like she always does when I get too deep.

I kiss the center of it before guiding both her hands to my back. "Confía en mí, no voy a lastimarte." I caress the side of her face. "I promise, I won't hurt you."

RayVen kisses me softly and I take her silent cue to keep going. I was eight inches deep when her nails start to claw up my skin again. Slowly, I grind my way deeper into her body. She grabs a handful of my hair, gritting her teeth as she fights to take it. Slowly but surely, RayVen surrenders her body to me. The raw heat from her pussy engulfs my shaft; scorching my skin with each deep stroke. I hit her spot strong causing those flames to be extinguished by the flood of her juices. Listening to my wife's pleasure filled screams while I deep stroke them warm, slippery walls...I swear ain't no better feeling than this shit.

"This my pussy," I tell her. "Don't you ever give my shit away."

"I won't," she whispers.

"Di que es mío," I'm looking dead in her eyes now.

"It's yours...Xavien," she tells me with no hesitation. "I don't want to lose you."

I kiss her then. Why'd she have to say that shit? I wasn't tryna think about nothing else. Being deep inside my wife is the only thing that matters right now. Pushing her legs back, I stand strong in that pussy. Her eyes roll up in her head as my strokes get stronger. If I was gonna die, then let it be right now. At least I'll go out with a good memory. At least I'll be with the person I love the most. Even in the darkness I can see tears streaming down her face. RayVen locks her arms around my shoulders, holding me close to her as them walls get sloppy as a muthafucka. I keep hitting that shit until I release what feels like a month's worth of nut deep inside her.

"FUUUCKK!!!" I swear it takes damn near five minutes for me to finish.

Both of us are still holding onto each other even after we had both calmed down. I can look in her eyes and tell she is just as worried about losing me as I am about losing her. Ain't shit promised in this life. But I'm gonna do what I gotta do to come back to this woman. Or at least make sure she's safe. I kiss my wife for what seems like hours. RayVen locks her legs around me as she continues to rub my back. Slowly but surely, we both fall asleep with me deep inside her.

CHAPTER 25

RayVen

There's no fighting the smile on my face when I wake up the next morning and feel Xavien's arms wrapped snugly around my waist. It seems like the world around me finally made sense again. The war that has been raging in my heart and my mind was silenced by that first touch from him. I swear, last night was amazing on so many levels. For a moment, I allow myself to fantasize about the events of last night. It had been too long since I felt my husband inside of me, and I wasn't about to wait a moment longer. While he went to get the shower ready, I undressed, attempting to ignore the pain in my leg. But when he picked me up and carried me, I was like no pain, no gain. I know God got tired of me calling on Him last night, but Xavien's stroke game is lethal. My poor kitty cat lost all nine of its lives last night, but that man kept bringing it back to life. True, my body is sore as hell right now, but I wouldn't have it any other way. I missed every—and I do mean EVERY—bit of my husband. But I know his passion for me last night was more than just make up sex.

As I lie here, I can't help thinking about everything he told me last night about being set up. Suddenly, there's no denying the guilt over how I acted towards him. If only I'd taken time to listen to what he had to tell me that day. I was so angry and so quick to believe he'd cheated on me. Then there was everything about this confrontation between him and this dude Nolo. From what I saw at the farmer's market, Nolo isn't strong enough to hurt Xavien unless he has some back up. Regardless, I will not lose Xavien to this bullshit. I refuse to lose my husband to this. Someway, somehow, I'm going to figure out a way to help him. I glance at the clock and decide to cook some breakfast for us. But when I try to slide out of bed, his arm tightens its grip around my waist.

"About time you woke up," Xavien tells me.

I can't help giggling when he snuggles his face in my neck. "How long have you been awake?"

"Long enough to check on X and watch yo' sexy ass sleep."

I start to blush.

"Before I forget, there's something I've been meaning to give you."

He lets me go momentarily and begins to search through the nightstand. I wrap the sheet around myself as I sit up in bed. When he finally turns around, I notice the small ring box in his hand. He opens it and I damn near fall out of bed.

"Xavien…shut up!" I say as I stare at the huge diamond in the 14K white gold ring.

He laughs as he takes my hand and slides it on my finger. "I thought I'd give it an upgrade, you feel me. Ain't that what dudes do when they fuck up?"

"Oh my god…" I can't stop staring at it. "It's so beautiful. I don't deserve this."

"How about miss me with that shit."

I shake my head. "Xavien I was mad at you for nothing. I should have—"

He silences me with a kiss. "Look Ray, both of us did and said shit we ain't mean. But since we are apologizing, I'm sorry for laying hands on you the way I did. There ain't no excuse for that shit." He shakes his head. "I ain't want you to think that—"

"I don't. He wasn't half the man you are so I can't even put the two of you in the same category."

He nods. "But for the record, I ain't fuck around on you with Marianna. Way back in the day when I was still running the streets I admit, I used to fuck with her. That was some shit in my past that I buried cuz it wasn't that deep. But I shoulda kept it one hunnid when I realized who she was."

"Yeah, you definitely should have. Maybe I would've beat her ass a little sooner."

"What you mean by that?"

I go on to tell him everything about that day Marciano came by to give money to Tim. And the slick shit Marianna came out her mouth with which caused me to jump on her ass.

Surprisingly, he starts laughing. "Damn, I hate I missed that shit."

"Yeah…but now, I'm out of a job." I rest my head on his shoulder when he wraps his arm around me. "I really miss my kids, X."

"Baby, you don't need to work for that bullshit center to do what you love. When all this shit is handled you need to open up your own shit, that way you can make sure they good."

My eyes grow to the size of saucers. I'm shocked by what he just said. "Xavien...are you serious?"

"Fuck yeah, I'm serious. Just like you pushed me to get my business popping, I'm pushing you to do the same shit. Fuck that muthafucka Mitchell. I'm sure your co workers would rather work for you anyway."

I laugh then. "X, I don't know anything about running a business."

"Did I?" he responds. "Baby, quit that shit. You smart as hell and you gotta big heart...that's why yo' titties so big."

I hit him with a pillow causing him to laugh. "Shut up!"

"Nah, but real talk. I believe in you, Ray. I've heard you talk about improving that place since you been there. And I feel like all those dreams you have should be used in your own spot, not someone else's."

I'm smiling from ear to ear at this point. To have Xavien believe in me the way he does is more than I could ever ask for. Before I can thank him, there's a soft knock on the door which grabs our attention. Xavien jumps out of bed to open it and X comes running in the room.

"Good morning!" he says.

Xavien scoops him up. "Dude, how did you get out of your crib?"

X starts laughing. "I climb."

We can only shake our heads. This child never ceases to amaze us.

"Guess it's time to get you a bigger bed, huh?"

"Yeah, I big boy."

Xavien puts him on the bed next to me since his legs were too short to climb up. "Mommy?"

"Yes, sweet pea."

"We stay here with Daddy now?"

I look over at Xavien and smile. "Yes, sweet pea, we're staying."

"YAY!!!"

After we are all cleaned up and full of breakfast, I get a call from Ty saying he's about to be discharged from the hospital. Can our day possibly get any better? With all the discharge paperwork and talking to the nurse about scheduling his follow up appointments, it takes close to forty-five minutes to get him to Xavien's truck. Ty was trying to be tough by wanting to walk down but I made his hard-headed behind ride in a wheelchair. Of course, X hopped in with him for a ride to the lobby. While on the way home, we stopped by Dad's house to get mine and X's clothes.

"I see you're finally listening to an old man," Dad says with a smirk when I bring the last of our bags from downstairs.

"Yeah, yeah…you end up being right sometimes," I tell him as I give him a hug.

"I just told X I want you all to take care of each other and stop letting this foolishness come between you. It should make you fight harder for each other. Not tear you apart."

I nod as I look towards the truck to see Xavien putting X in his seat. "We will, Dad. I'll check in with you soon as I can."

When we finally arrive home, I see V.J.'s Hummer along with Tony's parked in our yard. They must have come by soon as we left to pick up Ty. We'd barely gotten through the front door when savory smells from the kitchen began to waft through the air. I guess Ms. Lana couldn't wait for us to get home.

"Damn, finally I can get some real food!" Ty says excitedly.

"How about you sit down somewhere and rest," I tell him.

Since X is beginning to doze off, I take him upstairs to his room for a nap. We'd gotten something to eat while we were out, so he will be fine until later on. When I finally make it down I hear Xavien on the phone.

"Yeah, I know where that is," he says to someone. I watch as he nods and ends the call.

The expression on my husband's face when he ended the call was one I didn't recognize. There is this menacing, damn near evil look in his eyes that sends a chill through me. He nods at his brothers and they leave out the house without a word.

I run over to him. "Xavien, what's going on?"

He grabs me around the waist, kissing me long and deep.

"X…?"

"I'm going to put an end to this shit," he says finally. "Promise me you gonna stay here."

I shake my head in defiance. "No…Xavien let me help…"

"Fuck Ray, just do that for me aight! Please, don't leave this house until this shit is over…At least if I don't make it back I'll know y'all are taken care of."

Tears begin to cascade down my cheeks. "Xavien, I will not say goodbye to you so don't you dare say that shit to me."

He caresses the side of my face. "I love you, Ray."

I wrap my arms around him, silently begging him to stay. Wishing that I could shield him from those who wanted to take him away from me. Xavien gently pulls my arms from around his neck.

"Stop that shit," he says, gently wiping the tears from my face.

"I love you, Xavien."

I watch helplessly as he turns away from me and walks out the front door. As I watch him leave with his brothers, I can't help thinking about the first time I told him I loved him. It felt like déjà vu all over again. Only this time, he said it first. That night my heart broke because after that night, I didn't see him again until I moved here. Before then, I thought that would be the last time I ever laid eyes on him. And now, as the truck disappears out of sight, I have a feeling that this will be the last time I see my husband.

CHAPTER 26

Xavien

"X, you cool?" Carmine asks.

"I'm straight," I reassure him.

Marciano had finally hit me up with the spot to squash this shit once and for all. The building we're meeting him at is on the back end of the city. Some kinda abandoned train station or some shit. I ain't really give a fuck though. As long as all these muthafuckas are buried by the end of the night, I'm cool. But I was lying when I told my bro I was straight. Don't get it twisted, ain't no fear in my heart over what's about to go down. I been living reckless the majority of my life. Back when I was in the life, I never gave a fuck if I got smoked or not. As long as I took the muthafuckas with me, then I had the last laugh. Plus, I knew mom dukes was straight. It's been a good minute since she left me, but I still think about her from time to time. I know she would've loved RayVen. And woulda been spoiling the shit out of X. A part of me still wishes there was something I coulda done to save her. Maybe if I woulda just let her cook for me that night or taken her to a different spot for her birthday. Then maybe she would've still been here. But

235

bodying the muthafuckas who took her out is how I met RayVen in the first place. I swear, it's crazy how shit works sometimes. I may have fucked up with protecting mom dukes, but I'll be damn if I let them muthafuckas hurt my wife and my son.

While staring out the window, I think about the look on RayVen's face when I left out the house. I hated to see those tears in her eyes. And the last thing I wanted to do is leave her or X behind. Trust me, I'd rather be at the house chilling with my family. But all this shit has taught me that it ain't all about me. My job is to make sure they can move through life protected and that's what the fuck I'm gonna do. I feel my phone vibrating and I see a message from Tony.

Just posted up at the house, fam. Everybody's cool.

Appreciate you, I text back and put my phone back in my pocket.

A good minute later, we pull up to this raggedy ass building. The metal on the outside is rusted as fuck and the majority of the windows have been busted out. The area around it is dark as fuck except for the lights on the inside. We pull around to the entrance to see Marciano's Expedition along with three other cars.

"Looks like the muthafucka brought some backup," Carmine says.

"What, you scared nigga?" V.J. asks, clowning him.

"Nah, but if shit goes sour…whoever's left standing gotta make sure Mama is straight. Along with Ray and X," Carmine tells us. He must've started thinking the same shit I was earlier.

V.J. nods. "The old man always told us to ride together no matter what. So fuck it, let's ride this muthafucka 'til the wheels fall off."

I wasn't in the mood for this sentimental shit, so I hop out the Hummer and head to the trunk. Once my gun is locked and loaded I head inside with my brothers close behind me. When we're a little deeper in the building, I see Marciano standing on top of the staircase.

"Glad you can make it, Chains," he says. "For a minute I thought you weren't going to take us up on our invitation."

"I ain't come here to do all this talking muthafucka," I tell him.

"You're quite right. Well I'm a man of my word." He turns and motions for someone to come to him. Then I see Nolo's punk ass comes out the office behind him.

I start up the stairs towards them but three dudes come out of nowhere with their guns drawn on me. If those muthafuckas expected me to flinch they had me confused with the wrong nigga.

"If y'all muthafuckas wanna shoot me, then do it," I tell them.

"Now Chains, do you think I would've went through all this just to shoot you?" Marciano shakes his head. "From what my nephew tells me, y'all never got a chance to settle up one-on-one. My guys here are just a little insurance to make sure this is a fair fight."

"Unc, cut the bullshit man!" Nolo says. "Stick with the script; go ahead and drop this dude."

"Nah muthafucka, you wanna hide behind the phone and shit. I'm right here nigga. Square up." I toss my gun to the ground and step back to the center of the room.

"Aight then Puto!" Nolo throws down his jacket and comes running down the stairs.

Once I peep everybody in the room, I see that Marciano's squad is actually about eight deep, including the dudes who had drawn their guns on me. They all circle around us as we get ready to throw hands. I don't know why this muthafucka thought I was playing with his ass, because he was still running his fuckin' mouth.

"How does it feel nigga?" Nolo asks. "You thought you ended me back in Jersey. You thought you was the shit. But you missed yo' mark muthafucka. How does it feel to know that I single-handedly fucked up yo' life?"

I was through talking so I let him keep running his mouth.

"Ain't got shit to say now, huh? Big, bad Chains finally about to get dropped." He laughs. "Don't worry homes, after I end yo' ass. I'ma go to that nice ass house you got, kick the door in, and stick my dick in yo' fine ass wife. I wanna see how that phat ass feels when I hit that shit from the back."

I run over and drive my fist through that muthafuckas jaw. He staggers backwards, causing me to grab the back of his head and ram him face first into one of the wooden posts. Nolo falls to the ground but I snatch him up by the back of his shirt. My mind was so focused on killing the muthafucka that I didn't see when he grabbed a two-by-four off the ground. He swings and catches me in the stomach with it, knocking the wind out of me a little bit. Out the corner of my eye, I see him raise it over his head to break it across my back. I shake that shit off and catch that nigga in his throat. He doubles over holding his neck and I jump on his ass. Marciano must have gotten pissed off by how things were going 'cause next thing I know I hear him yelling.

"AYUDARLO, PENDEJOS!!"

Suddenly, his crew tries to jump me, but Carmine and V.J. start throwing hands too. While Nolo's on the floor bleeding and shit, a big ass brawl has broken out between us and his crew. If somebody wanted to see a good fight all they had to do is pull up to this building, because bodies were flying all over this muthafucka.

"Fuck this shit!" I heard one of the dudes say and I see him reach for a gun.

I uppercut him in the ribs, before putting the barrel of the gun in his mouth and squeezing the trigger. Somebody hits me across the back with a lead pipe and I drop to one knee. Another gun goes off and I see two more of Nolo's boys hit the floor with blood leaking out of them. Once I'm back on my feet, I see my bros were dropping bodies left and right. While they had me covered on that end, I grab hold of Nolo and continue to lay hands on him. With every blow from my fist, I think about the hell this muthafucka created in my life this past month. From almost destroying my business, for sending Ty to the hospital and almost taking him out, and for being dumb enough to think he can lay hands on my wife and get away with it. Nah, bruh, ain't no way I'm letting this muthafucka walk outta here breathing.

"X, look out!" I turn in time to see Carmine jump in front of me to take the bullet Marciano fired in my direction. He falls to the ground holding his shoulder.

I snatch Carmine's gun with the quickness and fire two shots at Marciano. One catches him in the chest while the other catches him in the middle of his forehead. As soon as his body drops, Nolo's bitch ass jumps on my back.

He tries to break my neck with some weak ass choke hold. "DIE! YOU MUTHAFUCKA! DIE!!!" Nolo screams.

I flip his ass off me and onto the floor. He staggers towards me trying to swing at me, but I shove my fingers into his neck and rip his throat out. Blood gushes from the hole in his neck as his body drops to the floor. I throw his torn flesh on the floor next to him. My eyes survey the inside of the building looking at the carnage we caused. I see Marciano's dead body hanging over the railing and a bunch of dead muthafuckas scattered all over the floor.

"Ah shit!" The sound of Carmine's voice brings me back to reality.

"Fam, you good?" I ask. He's leaning next to a barrel holding his shoulder.

I start to help V.J. get him to his feet, when out of nowhere I hear a gun firing several times behind me.

"What the fuck…"

It feels like somebody poured a gallon of hot lava in the center of my chest. I look down and my white shirt is soaked in blood. It takes a minute for me to realize that I'd been shot. I had to lay eyes on this muthafucka. But my knees give out from under me, preventing me from turning around. I hear Carmine and V.J. yelling my name but I can't seem to move. Everything around me gets blurry as fuck when I hit the ground. But when I look up, there's no mistaking that bitch Marianna standing over me with her gun smoking.

"I guess you'll have no choice but to remember me now, cuz I'm gonna be the last bitch you see, nigga." She smirks at me as she raises the barrel towards my head.

Even though it's obvious this bitch is about to smoke me, all I can think about is RayVen and X. I guess all them muthafuckas was right when they say your life passes before your eyes when you're on your way out. 'Cause I see myself hustling on the street as a kid. Arguing with my mom. Then I see the night she died in my arms. The five years I spent in prison. I ain't never been on no bitch shit, but a tear falls from my eyes when visions of me and RayVen begin to flash in my head. From that first time I met her in the prison and how she blew my mind. The way she screams my name when I make love to her. I see that day on the beach in Puerto Rico when I made her my wife. How beautiful she looked when she gave birth to my son. It's fucked up that I'll never get to see my lil' dude grow up or hold my wife in my arms again. I hope my bros cancel that bitch and keep their word to look out for my family. The next thing I hear is a gun firing again and everything around me goes dark.

CHAPTER 27

$\mathcal{I}$'ve been pacing back and forth since Xavien left. Although Ms. Lana helped me by feeding X and fixing a plate for Ty, I couldn't bring myself to eat anything. I know I promised Xavien I would stay here but I wouldn't be able to live with myself if I didn't try to help him.

"Fuck it," I say out loud as I go to my purse to get my gun. After checking the mag to make sure it is full, I stick it in the back of my pants and head towards the door.

"Ma...where you going?" I turn around to see Ty walking towards me.

"I'm going to help Xavien."

He nods. "Please be careful, Ma."

I give him a quick kiss on the forehead and head out the front door.

Tony jumps out of his truck as soon as he sees me walking out. "Ray, what you doing?"

"Do you know where Xavien went?" I ask him.

"Yeah, but Ray...X told me..."

"I know Tony, but he needs me. I got this feeling that he's in trouble," I tell him. "Please, take me to where he is."

He and Enzo exchange glances. Then he nods. "Aight, hop in."

After I jump in the back, we speed down the road. It takes about twenty minutes for us to reach a dirt road on the far end of the city. We follow it for about ten more minutes until we reach this old broken-down building. For some reason it reminds me of something out of a horror film. It's extremely dark out but there's no mistaking V.J.'s Hummer. I waste no time jumping out.

"Hold up Ray, you don't know what's popping off," Tony tells me.

As we approach the door we hear gunshots and there's no mistaking Carmine and V.J. yelling.

"NOOO!!! X!!"

"Xavien..."

I take off running, ignoring Tony and Enzo as they call for me to come back. When I reached the inside of the building it feels as if the beating of my heart stopped for a moment. I don't think there is a word to describe the rage I feel welling up inside me when I see Xavien collapse to the floor after that bitch shot him. Seems like the fires of hell had risen up around me as I grab my gun from my pants and fire it at Marianna. Even with the tears blurring my vision, a bullet catches her in the shoulder. I don't even give her the chance to turn around. Running towards her, I tackle her to the ground. She attempts to shoot at me but I hit her in the face with the butt of my gun. Not once, not twice but repeatedly. Before long she's unconscious, but I can't stop hitting her. The more blood flies from that bitch, the more I hit her across the face.

"RayVen stop!"

I recognize Carmine's voice but I can't seem to stop swinging my arm. I swear to God if she's taken Xavien away from me, I will travel to the depths of hell to draw more blood from this bitch.

Carmine eventually grabs my arms to stop me. "Ray, if we don't get X to a doctor ASAP he's not gonna make it."

I allow him to pull me to an upright position then I take my gun and shoot that bitch in the head. Once I see the blood leaking from that bitch's skull I collapse to my knees next to Xavien. There is so much blood covering his shirt and he doesn't appear to be breathing. I hadn't realized how bad he was hurt until now.

"NOOOOO!!!! XAVIEN, DON'T YOU DARE LEAVE ME!" I began to sob uncontrollably.

I had no idea Tony and Enzo made it into the room until one of them carries me to V.J.'s Hummer. It takes both of them to load Xavien in the back with me. I rest his head on my lap, cradling him as close to me as possible. With my hand on his chest, I'm able to feel his soft, shallow breaths. I lean down and kiss his forehead gently.

"Hold on, baby," I tell him. "We're going to get you some help. Just please hold on."

A few seconds pass and I hear the doors slam up front. "Yo, we need you ASAP," I hear V.J. say to someone.

I look up to see he's on his phone.

"It's X; he's hurt pretty bad…Aight we'll be there in a few."

Once he hung up, he hauls ass away from the building. As soon as we're far enough I hear an explosion behind us. I turn around to see the building is now on fire and Tony's truck racing to catch up with us. It seems like an eternity passes before we reach a large home in a suburban neighborhood. There's a camera on the outside gate that seems to scan the Hummer when we pull up. It blinks green, causing the gates to swing open. V.J. drives to the back of the house where an elderly man is standing outside waiting. Tony and Enzo waste no time hopping out of their truck to come take Xavien inside. I follow closely behind them to a room that has an operating table and a bunch of medical tools. Two other men rush past me and into the room. I watch as they put an oxygen mask on Xavien and begin to cut away his shirt.

"RayVen, let's wait in the living room ok," Carmine says.

I don't have the energy to fight him as he ushers me to the other room. He helps me get situated on the couch before disappearing back down the hall.

Something starts vibrating on my leg, causing me to reach in my pocket to get my phone. It's a text from Ty.

Ma, you good? Is Big X okay?

My hands are shaking so badly but I manage to respond. *I'm holding up as good as I can. Xavien was hurt pretty badly.*

Fuck! Is he talkin' at all?

Tears start falling down my face again. *No, sweetheart. He's barely breathing.*

:(What hospital y'all at? I can get Grandpa to bring us there.

Please, just stay with X and Ms. Lana ok. I'll be home soon as I can.

:(Okay Mama.

After putting my phone away, I sit in the living room with my mind racing. I stare down at my clothes, which were covered in my husband's blood. A cold shiver runs through me as the sight of him lying on the concrete floor with blood seeping through his shirt runs through my memory. If only I'd gotten there sooner, maybe he would be ok. Please God, let him be okay. I grab a nearby blanket and curl up on the couch.

I don't know how much time has passed before I feel a hand on my shoulder, stirring me awake. It's the same elderly gentleman who was waiting outside for us earlier.

"Go back to sleep. I was just checking on you."

"How's Xavien?" I ask ignoring his comment.

"We were able to remove all the bullets. They missed his heart and spinal column. A few inches further and he would have been either dead or paralyzed. We have him cleaned up and stabilized. Only time will tell if he pulls through or not."

"Can I see him, please?"

He nods and I follow him upstairs.

A part of me literally dies when I walk in the room and see my husband lying in bed with bandages over his torso. I sit down on the king-sized bed next to him, being careful not to sit on the IV that's hooked up to him. Taking his hand in mine I bring it to my lips and kiss it softly. I caress his face and notice his eyes fluttering gently but they don't open.

"Xavien...I know you can hear me...X, I need you to fight through this." I feel a lump swelling in my throat and I swallow it back. "Remember what you said in the hospital when X was born... You promised me...you promised you would never leave me. Your son needs you. And baby I need you too... I can't continue this life knowing that you're not here to share it with me...Please wake up and come back to us."

I lean down to kiss him softly on the lips. But unlike the fairytale, he doesn't open his eyes. He just lies there breathing softly, dangling dangerously between life and death. I just want to argue with him one more time. Have him hold me in his arms. See that devilish smile of his. Have him whisper in my ear as he makes love to me all night. I lean down resting my head on his chest. His breathing is so shallow.

A soft knock on the door grabs my attention and I see Carmine standing in the doorway. "Doc needs to come in and check his bandages. I can give you a ride home."

I shake my head. "Carmine, I can't just leave him here."

"I promised Chains I'd look out for you and make sure your son is ok. I can't go back on my word."

Reluctantly, I agree to go home. I give Xavien one more kiss until I see him again.

"He's in very good hands, trust me."

When I finally make it home, Ty and Ms. Lana are up sitting

in the living room. She covers her mouth and begins to weep when she sees the large amount of blood on my clothes. Ty runs up to me, hugging me as tightly as he's able to. Eventually I'm able to give them the short version of what happened tonight and tell them all we can do is pray for the best. Once in my room, I remove my clothes and step into a hot shower. With the water on full blast, I release everything I'm feeling inside. I scream, I cry and cry until nothing else would come out. After thirty minutes or so, I'm able to pull myself together enough to check on my son. I pick him up and carry him to my room. He was snoring lightly and I have no doubt he's fine, but I just needed to be near him. The only thing that brings me comfort is knowing my baby is safe and too young to know what's going on. X snuggles closer to me and I wrap my arm around him, attempting to fall asleep.

*****

Almost three weeks have passed since Xavien was injured. Carmine told me we have to keep things low-key until the investigation of the building that caught fire is over. The police are investigating all possible leads since Marciano and Marianna were reported missing. From what I saw on the news recently, they were ruling it as some kind of turf war gone wrong. I don't know what Enzo and Tony did to clean up everything, but whatever it is it worked. The only downside is I couldn't visit Xavien until the coast was clear. Carmine's being secretive about how things are going with him, so I don't know if that's a good or bad sign.

The following Friday, I finally receive a text from Carmine.

Yo Ray, everything's cool on our end.

Thank God, is Xavien ok?

I'd rather talk to you about that in person. Is it ok if I come by?

Yeah, I'll be upstairs with X more than likely.

Okay, see you in a few.

With Ty in his room playing his video game and Ms. Lana watching TV, I decide to get X ready for bed. He allows me to give him a bath but when I put him to bed, he decides he wants to play instead of sleep.

My phone buzzes and it's another text from Carmine.

Are you upstairs?

Yeah, in X's room.

I try covering him up but he kicks the cover off and bursts out laughing.

I shake my head and start tickling him. "Why you have to start with me tonight, huh?"

He continues to giggle.

"You gonna go to sleep for me?"

"No!" He stands up in his crib and starts bouncing up and down.

"Xavier DaeSean…"

He sits down immediately. "Mommy…where Daddy?"

I fight back tears. "He's not here, sweet pea."

"Daddy not here?"

I shake my head. "No baby, he's not."

"You got that shit wrong, baby," I hear from behind me. "Daddy's right here."

My knees give out from under me as I collapse on the floor and begin to cry. The sound of his voice is music to my ears. A pair of strong arms wrap around me and I didn't have to see his face to know my husband is finally home. But I look up anyway, taking in the sight of those green eyes staring back at me. I wrap my arms around his neck when he lifts me up in his arms and kisses me several times.

"Daddy! Daddy!" X squeals over and over again.

Xavien picks him up with one hand, embracing both of us tightly. I bury my face in his chest and continue to weep with joy, thanking God over and over again that he is home and one hundred percent healed.

EPILOGUE

Xavien

Three months later...

After all the bullshit that popped off with our family a few months ago, it's safe to say that all of us needed a fuckin' vacation. And I do mean all of us. So, I rented this nice ass beach house in Hawaii and we hauled ass. Plus, this is the first time X had seen the beach. I think it was a first for Ty too 'cause soon as he saw all those females in bikinis, lil' dude was gone. I think it's safe to say he's one hundred percent now. And speaking of which, so am I. The doctors were shocked by how quick I healed from those gunshots. But I wasn't gonna let them muthafuckas take me out like that. They tried like hell though. But I had a reason to keep fighting. I know nobody will ever believe me but when I was out, I swear I was talking to my mama and Armateo. Can't really say if I was dreaming or what, but that shit was so real. My mom told me that she loved me and was proud of me. And to stop blaming myself for what happened to her. Armateo told me if I threw in the towel he was gonna kick my ass. Next thing I know I was in a room

253

hooked up to IVs and shit. Once I realized that I was still alive the first thing I said was, where's Ray?

The doctor who'd patched me up called Carmine and he told me everything that went down. After he told me RayVen was cool, I started fighting to get back to her. When I was good, I told Carmine to let me use his phone to text her. I know she was worried about me and I wanted to surprise her ass. That night I walked in the room and saw her trying to get X to go to bed, I silently thanked God for allowing me to make it home to them. I was still kinda sore but soon as X went to sleep, I fucked the shit out of my wife. Shit, my dick wasn't hurt. And I needed to remind her I wasn't going nowhere. I look over towards the house and see RayVen running inside. Then Mama Armateo going in after her.

What the fuck are those two up to?

RayVen

As the toilet flushes, I take a cold washcloth and dab it over my face. I look in the mirror and notice my eyes are red and watery, causing me to run more cold water over the cloth. Once my eyes are a little clearer, I close the lid on the toilet and have a seat. My hands start trembling as I reach for the test stick off the counter and read the results. It's a good thing I'm sitting down because I probably would have collapsed. I blink my eyes once. Twice. And a third time. But the results remained the same. A soft knock on the door causes me to wrap the test in some toilet paper and throw it away.

"One second," I tell the person on the other side as I wash my hands.

When I finally open the door, I'm surprised to see Ms. Lana standing in front of me.

"Are you okay, my dear?"

"Mm hmm…yes ma'am. I'm ok." I'm lying of course.

She takes my hand gently and walks me to the kitchen.

"RayVen…are you pregnant?"

I'd just found out, how in the hell did she know?

"I…I…" I can't think of a lie so I just nod.

Ms. Lana embraces me tightly. "Ohh…I knew it." When she pulls away from me I notice she's crying. "Look at you, you look so beautiful."

"Mama don't do that." I fan my face trying to shoo away my tears.

"I'm so happy." She rubs my stomach gently. "She's going to be so beautiful."

"Mama, I'm not even showing yet." I shake my head. "How do you know?"

She wipes her eyes again. "I just know."

Suddenly, we hear Dad yelling that the food is ready. We grab everything from the inside and get things set up on the picnic table. After everyone has made it to the table, we all join hands so Dad can bless the food.

"What were you two inside gossiping about?" Dad asks us.

Ms. Lana only smiles.

"RayVen, would you like to tell us something?"

"Yeah, this chicken is blazing," I say, causing everyone to burst out laughing.

"That's funny...can someone explain why I had a dream about swimming with fish?"

For some reason everybody turned to looked at Ty, who is chowing down on some ribs.

He stops when he notices everyone is looking at him. "Oh, y'all got jokes...hell no it ain't me!"

Carmine and V.J. both looked at the ladies who were with them. They both laugh and deny being pregnant.

"RayVen, you over there glowing like a Christmas tree…" Dad points out.

Xavien rubs my back, causing me to look at him. "Baby?"

I only nod, causing him to jump up from the table and spin me around.

"Yo X, you gonna be a big brother," Ty tells him.

"Yay!!" he yells in response.

"Baby, why you ain't tell me?" Xavien asks.

I laugh. "Because I just found out."

He kisses me then. "I love you, baby. Like I said from the beginning, I ain't never leaving you."

"You promise?"

He places my hand on his heart. "I promise."

Xavien and I go back to the table to enjoy our dinner with our family. As the sun begins to set in the horizon, I thank God that the past is finally dead and buried. Here's to a new beginning and peace in our future.

THE END

Looking for a publishing home?

Royalty Publishing House, Where the Royals reside, is accepting submissions for writers in the urban fiction genre. If you're interested, submit the first 3-4 chapters with your synopsis to submissions@royaltypublishinghouse.com.

Check out our website for more information: www.royaltypublishinghouse.com.

Text ROYALTY to 42828 to join our mailing list!

To submit a manuscript for our review, email us at
submissions@royaltypublishinghouse.com

Text RPHCHRISTIAN to 22828 for our
CHRISTIAN ROMANCE novels!

Text RPHROMANCE to 22828 for our
INTERRACIAL ROMANCE novels!

Get LiT!

Download the LiTeReader app today and enjoy exclusive content, free books, and more

Do You Like CELEBRITY GOSSIP?

Check Out QUEEN DYNASTY!
Visit Our Site: www.thequeendynasty.com